Amy Cross is the author of more than 250 horror, paranormal, fantasy and thriller novels.

OTHER TITLES BY AMY CROSS INCLUDE

1689
American Coven
Angel
Anna's Sister
Annie's Room
Asylum
B&B
Bad News
The Curse of the Langfords
Daisy
The Devil, the Witch and the Whore
Devil's Briar
Eli's Town
Escape From Hotel Necro
The Farm
Grave Girl
The Haunting of Blackwych Grange
The Haunting of Nelson Street
The House Where She Died
I Married a Serial Killer
Little Miss Dead
Mary
One Star
Perfect Little Monsters & Other Stories
Stephen
The Soul Auction
Trill
Ward Z
Wax
You Should Have Seen Her

THE HAUNTING OF STYRE HOUSE

THE SMYTHE TRILOGY BOOK ONE

AMY CROSS

This edition
first published by Blackwych Books Ltd
United Kingdom, 2024

2

Copyright © 2024 Blackwych Books Ltd

All rights reserved. This book is a work of fiction.
Names, characters, places, incidents and businesses are
the product of the author's imagination or are
used fictitiously. Any resemblance to actual persons,
living or dead, or to actual events or locations,
is entirely coincidental.

Also available in e-book format.

www.amycross.com
www.blackwychbooks.com

CONTENTS

PROLOGUE
page 15

CHAPTER ONE
page 19

CHAPTER TWO
page 29

CHAPTER THREE
page 39

CHAPTER FOUR
page 49

CHAPTER FIVE
page 57

CHAPTER SIX
page 65

CHAPTER SEVEN
page 75

CHAPTER EIGHT
page 83

CHAPTER NINE
page 93

CHAPTER TEN
page 101

CHAPTER ELEVEN
page 109

CHAPTER TWELVE
page 119

CHAPTER THIRTEEN
page 129

CHAPTER FOURTEEN
page 137

CHAPTER FIFTEEN
page 145

CHAPTER SIXTEEN
page 153

CHAPTER SEVENTEEN
page 161

CHAPTER EIGHTEEN
page 169

CHAPTER NINETEEN
page 177

CHAPTER TWENTY
page 185

CHAPTER TWENTY-ONE
page 193

CHAPTER TWENTY-TWO
page 201

CHAPTER TWENTY-THREE
page 209

CHAPTER TWENTY-FOUR
page 217

CHAPTER TWENTY-FIVE
page 227

CHAPTER TWENTY-SIX
page 237

CHAPTER TWENTY-SEVEN
page 245

CHAPTER TWENTY-EIGHT
page 255

CHAPTER TWENTY-NINE
page 263

CHAPTER THIRTY
page 271

THE HAUNTING OF STYRE HOUSE

PROLOGUE

"SO HERE'S THE PLAN," she continued. "I'm going to get to the car. I'm not quite sure how, but I'm going to manage it somehow and I'm going to get the engine started. Then you're going to join me. If I have to distract whoever's out there, then I'll figure out a way to do that too. All *you* have to do, Mum, is run to the car when I tell you it's time. Do you think you can manage that?"

Reaching the door, she began to wonder why her mother had said nothing. She figured that perhaps Alison had simply fallen asleep, and when she stopped in the doorway and looked across the darkened hallway she saw that her mother was indeed sitting slumped in the chair.

"Okay, Mum," she said, taking a couple of

steps forward, "here's the -"

Stopping suddenly, she saw something moving between her mother's feet. Staring down at the dark mass, she couldn't quite figure it out at first, until finally she realized that her mother's intestines had been pulled out through a hole in her belly and were now dangling down to the floor, where Smythe was entangled in the various loops and tubes, playing with them as if they were nothing more than thick strands of string. As she stared at the horrific sight, watching the glistening intestines shaking in the moonlight, Parker could only try desperately to convince herself that somehow she was mistaken.

Looking up at her, while still wrapped in Alison's guts, Smythe let out a playful meow.

"Parker," Alison groaned, slowly managing to lift her head and look up at her daughter. "I think you might have been right. I think I'm... not doing too well."

"Mum -"

Before she could get another word out, Parker saw a shape approaching the frosted glass. She tried to call out, but in that moment the glass shattered, sending thick shards spinning across the hallway. One of the larger shards sliced straight through Alison's neck, severing her head and sending it tumbling down onto the floor, where it landed in the trail of intestines just as Smythe scurried out of the way.

Turning to look up at her, the cat – with blood caked around the sides of his face and pieces of flesh hanging from his fangs – let out an angry hiss.

CHAPTER ONE

Today...

"AND THIS," ALISON SAID, standing in front of the dilapidated old house and staring at the crumbling facade, "is our new home. Welcome to Styre House. Isn't it amazing?"

"It looks like it was hit by a bomb," her daughter Parker replied, clearly not sharing her enthusiasm. "It's falling apart. And what does Styre mean, anyway? What's a styre? It sounds a bit like sty. I suppose that'd be appropriate, because this place looks like somewhere only pigs would live. Pigs and losers with no other options."

"It's not that bad," Alison said with a sigh. "It's just in need of a little tender loving care, that's all. You need to learn to see the potential of a place, rather than fixating on how it looks right now. When I look at this house, do you know what I see? I see a glorious -"

Before she could finish, a metal sheet fell from the roof, landing with a clattering thud on the ground just a few feet away. Alison let out a shocked gasp and stepped back, but Parker merely remained in place and rolled her eyes. Somehow the falling metal sheet seemed to sum up her feelings about the move, certainly far better than words ever could.

"Exhibit A, Mum," she muttered finally. "Not content with falling apart, this wretched house is actually trying to fall apart *onto* us. The place should be condemned."

"Parker -"

"That was a literal attempt on our lives, Mum," she continued, turning to Alison. "If that metal sheet had fallen a little closer, it could have decapitated us both. Then again, at least that would've been a quick way to go."

"Stop being so... over the top. No-one's getting decapitated."

"You don't know that," Parker insisted. "Mum, it's not too late to turn back. It can't be." She looked around, but once again she saw nothing more than faded old scrub-land and a few half-collapsed outbuildings. "There must be some sort of cooling-off period. If you go back to the estate agent, you can fess up that you made a terrible mistake and they'll give you your money back. Then we can move home and live like normal people instead of... rural trash."

She turned to her mother again.

"Damn it," she added, "I just realized that's *exactly* what you're turning us into. We're turning into... country hobos!"

"You just need to get into the spirit of the venture," Alison said, putting an arm around her daughter and pulling her closer while once again looking at the derelict house. "Sure, it needs some work, but that's part of the charm. You know, good old-fashioned honest hard work never hurt anyone. It's actually really character-building, and one day you'll thank me for bringing you out here and helping you to connect with the great British countryside."

"Never," Parker said darkly. "I will *never* thank you for any of this, and do you know why? It's because this is a really bad, absolutely terrible, no good debacle of an idea." She paused, before kissing her mother on the cheek. "It's probably going to bankrupt us, and we'll have to live on the streets turning tricks for money! Seriously, Mum! You've ruined both our lives!"

***

"Oh wow!" Alison called out a few minutes later, her voice echoing through the empty house. "Sweetheart, come and look at the bedrooms! You're going to love them! Do you want to come and pick which one you like best?"

"Whichever one has the least number of cockroaches and bugs," Parker said under her breath as she walked across what she assumed was going to be the living room. Reaching the large windows at the far end, she looked outside and saw nothing but some old, large and very bare trees that had clearly known better days. Even the nature and wildlife surrounding Styre House seemed jaded and dead, as if the whole area had given up.

No, the whole county.

Or the whole country.

"I'll take the room I'm least likely to fall through the floor of," she added.

Feeling a buzzing sensation in her pocket, she pulled out her phone and saw a message from her friend Mary. She tapped to open the message, which turned out to be a general check-in to see how she was coping with the move.

"I hate this place," she typed quickly. "It's like we've gone back in time."

She tapped to send the message, only to see a small exclamation mark appear next to the status box.

"Great," she muttered, setting the phone on the windowsill. "That's really typical, isn't it? We're living in the middle of nowhere and we've barely even got any signal."

"Come up and look at this!" Alison yelled from the room above, as floorboards creaked almost directly above Parker's head. "I'm serious, you have to see it for yourself! This place is so beautiful!"

Another floorboard creaked, all the way over above the other end of the room.

"It stinks," Parker said, turning to look toward the hallway. "No wonder it was a -"

Stopping suddenly, she saw that she had a visitor. A black cat was slinking its way into the room, brushing against the door's jamb, letting its tail twitch and flick slightly as it padded across the floorboards. Surprised by the animal's arrival, Parker watched as the cat began to follow a path toward the far side of the room, as if it was keen to avoid getting too close. Finally the cat stopped and looked up at one of the other windowsills, before jumping up and then starting to purr as it looked out through the dirty glass panes.

"Well," Parker said after a few more seconds, "I wasn't expecting to find someone else already living here. How do you do?"

Making her way over, she peered at the cat's fur, which seemed clean enough. Reaching out, she cautiously began to stroke its back, and the purring sound continued as its tail flicked again.

"My name's Parker," she continued. "My utterly deluded mother bought this rundown old dump and now she thinks she's going to fix it up and turn it into a rural boutique hideaway for... I don't know, morons with more money than sense. Except that even the morons are going to have better offers, so I really don't know what Mum's planning to do except pour all of Dad's life insurance payout into -"

Stopping suddenly, she stroked the cat's back for a moment longer.

"Was that too much information?" she asked, before sighing and nodding. "Yeah, definitely too much information. You didn't come in here to be bored to death by my life story, did you? Even if it's an utterly tragic tale."

The cat looked up at her, watching her face with its yellow eyes.

"I'm glad to see that there's some life around here, though," Parker continued. "You know, I like dogs, but I've always been way more of a cat person. Hey, have you been mousing on the property? I bet you've been totally keeping the place clear of vermin, right? Honestly, Mum should thank you and give you some rewards. I'm sure the house would have been consumed by rats if you hadn't been here to keep tabs on them all. Then again, that might not be such a bad thing. If they'd chewed the house down, Mum and I wouldn't ever have come here in the first place." She leaned closer. "Bad cat!"

"Are you coming up?" Alison called out from the room above.

"I'm busy!" Parker shouted back at her.

"Doing what?"

"Come and see!" she yelled, still stroking the cat. "I'm sorry if we've crashed your party," she told the purring animal. "I bet you had this whole place set up as your own private pad, and now here we are to intrude. I'm sorry, it's really not my idea. Like I told you, Mum's behind all of this. If I'm honest, after Dad died she went a little nuts, and I suppose in some ways it's good that she's at least found some kind of focus." She began to scratch behind the cat's ears, which seemed to be a popular move. "There's nothing any of us can do to change the situation," she continued, as she heard her mother hurrying back down the stairs, "so we're just going to have to make the best of it for now. I'm fifteen, and as soon as I'm old enough to move out, I'm going to be gone like a flash."

"Parker," Alison said as she headed into the room, "you really ought to come up and see -"

In that moment, she froze as she saw her daughter petting the cat.

"Where did that thing come from?" she asked, stepping closer. Already she was scrunching her nose slightly, making no real effort to disguise her sense of disgust. "We never said anything about having pets. What's it doing here?"

"Beats me," Parker replied. "Is it possible that he came with the house and the land? You've got to admit, he seems pretty comfortable here. Almost like he owns the place."

"Be careful," Alison replied, clearly unimpressed. "It might have fleas."

"He doesn't have fleas."

"You don't know that," Alison continued. "Parker, we've got a lot of work to do here and it won't help to have some kind of... feral animal coming into the house and giving us both the plague."

Parker rolled her eyes.

"That's where the plague came from!" Alison insisted. "It came from fleas, which came from cats and other vermin. Darling, I'm sorry, I know you probably think that he's cute but you really need to look at the bigger picture."

"This cat's cleaner than anything else here," Parker pointed out, raising a skeptical eyebrow. "Mum, you've moved me hundreds of miles away from my friends and isolated me in a rickety old farmhouse that looks like it's come straight out of a horror movie. The least you can do is let me make friends with the local wildlife. Besides, I bet he's really good at catching mice and rats, and you just *know* there are loads of rodents hiding away in this place."

"It's not allowed in the kitchen," Alison said firmly, "or upstairs in the bedrooms."

"But he can hang out down here?"

"As long as it doesn't make a mess," Alison muttered, still unsettled and scrunching her nose up as she turned and headed out of the room. "I don't like it, but I'll give it a chance. One wrong move, though, and I'm getting one of those electric invisible fence things to keep it off the property. I really don't like the idea of some dirty stray animal wandering around in the house. And I want you to come up and look at the bedrooms, Parker. You've got to tell me which one you want before the furniture truck arrives."

She was still talking to herself as she headed up the stairs. Smiling, Parker watched for a moment as the cat nonchalantly licked one of his paws.

"Don't mind Mum," she muttered after a few seconds. "She's kinda highly-strung, but that's mainly because she's been through a lot. Stick around long enough and you might even start to like her. And I think the feeling might eventually be mutual."

Smiling, she made her way through to inspect the rest of the house. The cat, meanwhile, licked the back of his paw for a moment longer before stopping and turning to look over at the doorway. As footsteps rang out in both the kitchen and one of the bedrooms above, the cat sat completely still until finally – very slowly – his eyes began to narrow.

CHAPTER TWO

"WE'VE GOT SO MUCH work to do tomorrow," Alison complained later as she and Parker sat at either end of the dining room table, eating takeaway food from plastic containers. "All these boxes need unpacking."

"They don't all need unpacking in one day," Parker pointed out.

"They certainly do," Alison replied tensely. "You know, I don't think you quite understand the enormity of the task we're facing here. I've budgeted it all out, I've planned meticulously, and it only works if we get a move on. We've got a long summer of hard work ahead of us, my girl, and you need to accept that fact. If you think we're here for some kind of extended holiday, you can forget it."

"Trust me," Parker said, rolling her eyes, "*nothing* about this move struck me as being remotely like a holiday."

"And I don't need you being snippy," Alison added. "I need you to support me in this."

"Mum -"

"It's what your father would have wanted."

"Okay," Parker said under her breath, looking down at her beef and noodles, "way to pull the dead parent guilt trip on me."

"What did you say?"

"Nothing," she continued, looking back at her mother and forcing a smile. "You're right, I'm sure Dad would love seeing us sitting here right now in this hell-hole of a so-called house, having wagered our financial future on turning it into some kind of boutique hotel in the middle of nowhere. I'm sure he'd much prefer that, rather than us investing the money he left and just getting normal jobs like other people." She paused, fully aware that she was being a little harsh but finding herself unable to hold back. "Way to go, Mum."

"I don't like your tone," Alison said haughtily, no longer able to maintain eye contact. "If you didn't want to move here with me, you could always have gone to stay with your uncle Rich."

"You *never* told me that was an option,"

Parker replied. "Not once. If you had, don't you think I'd be in his spare room in Birmingham right now?"

"It's not too late," Alison told her. "Fine, abandon ship. See if I care. Believe me, I'm very much accustomed to people storming off and leaving me to manage on my own." She dabbed at one of her eyes with a handkerchief as tears began to gather. "It's been like that all my life and I should never have expected anything to change now. All I want to do is make something of myself instead of sitting around like some depressed widow, and I'm being attacked for it."

"Mum -"

"Enough!" Alison snapped angrily, slamming a fist against the table before getting to her feet. Seemingly shocked by her own outburst, she looked around for a moment before turning and storming out of the room. "I'm sorry, I'm not hungry," she stammered. "I think I'd like to go and rest in my room."

"Mum, come back!" Parker called out, before sighing as she heard her mother hurrying up the stairs. "Damn it," she added with a heavy sigh, leaning back in her chair and tossing her fork into the container. "I didn't mean it like that. I just miss my old life, that's all."

She waited for an answer.

Instead, she heard one of the bedroom doors slamming shut.

"That's daughter-of-the-year level behavior right there," she sighed. "Well done, Parker. Now you've made your widowed mother burst into tears. I hope you're satisfied."

***

Half an hour later, having waited as long as she could, Parker stopped outside one of the bedroom doors and listened to the sound of her mother sobbing. She took a deep breath and briefly considered walking away, before knocking gently and then bumping the door open to see her sitting on the bed.

"I'm fine," Alison said, wiping her eyes with another tissue. "Just finish your meal downstairs."

"You're not fine," Parker replied, heading over to the bed and plonking herself down, then putting an arm around her. "I'm sorry for being mean, Mum. I guess my frustrations boiled over, but I shouldn't have taken it out on you. I'm going to help around this place, I promise."

"Did you mean what you said?" Alison sniffled. "Do you really think that your father would be disappointed in me for buying this place?"

"No, of course not," Parker lied.

"And do you really want to go and live with your uncle?"

"Hell, no. He's kinda creepy, anyway."

"Because I know it's a big job," Alison continued, scrunching the tissue up and then looking around the room. "Believe me, I'm fully aware of the enormity of this entire project. I think I just wanted something to do, something that would take up my time and fill up my mind, something that would stop me constantly thinking about your father over and over again and..."

Her voice trailed off, and after a few seconds she burst into tears. Parker immediately pulled her closer, hugging her tight while feeling utterly awful for not having been more supportive.

"Dad would be so proud of you, you know," she said, before kissing the top of her mother's head. "He'd be amazed that you've got all these grand plans, and he'd do anything in his power to help you. He'd do that because it's the right thing, and it's what I'm going to do as well. I didn't mean it when I said I'd rather go and live with Uncle Rich, I was just being mean. We're going to get stuck in and by the end of summer we're going to have this place looking perfect. It'll be just like those sketches you showed me."

"Do you really think so?" Alison whimpered, sniffing back more tears.

"Are these the drawings?" Parker asked, reaching for a portfolio on the bed and pulling it closer, then opening it up to slide the various pages out. "They're so cool. You know, Mum, you're actually a very talented artist."

"Now I *know* you're blowing smoke up my bum," Alison sniffed, before watching for a moment as Parker leafed through some of the pages. "Do you really think so?"

"You've got a great way with light and color," Parker said, hoping that she sounded like she knew what she was talking about. "And shade."

She took a look at another drawing.

"How many bedrooms does this place have, anyway?" she continued. "I'm struggling a bit to get the layout straight."

"I watched a lot of art videos online," Alison told her, finally managing to force a smile despite the tears still running down her face. "I try not to take it too seriously, you know, but I've been experimenting with different techniques and trying to work out where my particular expertise rests. Do you really think I've got what it takes? I've been wondering whether, once the hotel's up and running,

I might get into painting a little more. I wouldn't expect to become hugely successful, of course, but I think I could submit my work to a few local galleries, and maybe to some in London as well."

"Mum -"

"I wouldn't be against having a show in London, either. Or Paris or New York at a push."

"Mum -"

"And I could hold little art courses here. Just little weekend retreats for like-minded people who want to develop their skills."

"I love your ambition," Parker said as she looked at more of the pages, "and your confidence. You know, I think -"

Before she could finish, she saw a copy of an old photo; the image clearly showed the house in better days, with several men standing outside the front. A handwritten scrawl in the top corner identified the year as 1907, which meant that the photo was more than a century old. Parker peered more closely at the half dozen men shown standing outside the front door, and she couldn't help but wonder what had happened to them; they were all fairly young, probably in their twenties, and she felt a shiver pass through her chest as she realized that just seven years later they'd likely all been shipped off to fight in the First World War.

She looked at the windows in the photo and tried to work out which of them looked out from her new bedroom.

"That'll be from some time back in the day," Alison said, sniffing back yet more tears. "Unmarried young gentlemen needed somewhere to stay while they were working, and before they found themselves wives. Do you think this was a boarding house? That'd be so fascinating!"

"I'll bet," Parker replied, still unable to shake a sense of sadness. "I wonder how many of them -"

Suddenly she stopped again as she spotted a dark smudge down near the bottom of the photo. She tilted her head slightly, and to her surprise she was just about able to make out a black cat in the image, with its eyes staring back out directly into the camera's lens. For a few seconds Parker felt as if the cat's intense gaze was almost looking directly into her soul, and she couldn't help but think back to the feline visitor who'd spent a short while in the house earlier and who'd then headed back outside and disappeared into the forest.

The similarity was striking.

"Looks like this place has always been popular with cats," she pointed out, trying to lighten the mood a little. "Hell, I wouldn't even be surprised if it's the same cat family. That one looks exactly like the little dude who popped by to welcome us earlier." She paused for a moment. "I hope he comes back. It'd be nice to have some life around the house."

CHAPTER THREE

WIND BLEW AGAINST STYRE House, causing the roof to creak slightly as Alison lay on her back in bed and stared up at the ceiling. She'd been exhausted all evening, yet as soon as her head had hit the pillow she'd suddenly stirred with all sorts of plans for the next day. Now she felt as if sleep was an impossible luxury.

Somewhere nearby, a chain briefly rattled, although this particular sound wasn't quite loud enough to penetrate Alison's consciousness.

Another gust of wind hit the building, bringing forth yet another loud creaking sound. Although she'd had the house surveyed before the purchase, Alison couldn't help worrying that the place might be a tad less solid than she'd been led to believe; she was even venturing into private conspiracy theories, worrying that the sellers might have handed the surveyor a bung to encourage certain omissions in the final report. Now, as her wide-awake brain continued to torture her attempts at sleep, she began to imagine the entire house getting blown away by an errant gust, leaving her and Parker with absolutely nothing.

The chain rattled again.

Taking a deep breath, Alison told herself that the house was probably sturdier than it seemed. Sure, the place looked pretty bad, but this was only its starting point. Soon she was going to give it a fresh lick of paint and everything would start to seem better. Besides, it was fairly old, so clearly it must have withstood more than its fair share of bad weather over the years. If it was going to fall down, wouldn't it have fallen down by now?

A moment later she heard a brief bumping sound. Without sitting up, she looked down the bed just in time to see that her bedroom door was gently swinging open.

Just more wind, she told herself. *This place is probably as leaky as a sieve.*

Looking at the ceiling again, she decided to make another concerted attempt to fall asleep. She knew she should probably get up and try to tire herself out some other way, or that she should perhaps read for a while, but she felt that she really just needed to empty her mind and force herself to rest. Sure enough, as she closed her eyes and took yet another deep breath, she felt as if her body was loosening a little, as if this time – after a couple of hours – she might finally be able to drift away into a nice relaxing dream.

And then, after a few more seconds, she felt a light impact on the foot of the bed.

Puzzled, she opened her eyes and looked down again, and she was startled to see that the black cat had returned. Standing down near Alison's feet, the cat briefly twitched his tail and let out a faint purr as he looked around, seemingly entirely comfortable and at home in the room. Although her first instinct was to kick the animal away, Alison told herself that she should probably try to be more accommodating; after all, her daughter clearly liked the cat and she wanted to give Parker a little lift, so she decided to at least try to tolerate the intrusion.

"Shoo," she whispered after a moment. "Parker's in the room opposite. You should go and curl up with her, she's more... animal-friendly."

She waited, but the cat merely stared at her. His tail looked a little stiff, twitching slightly, and after a moment he tilted his head to one side.

"I don't know what a twitching tail means," Alison said. "I don't understand your body language."

The cat offered no response.

"It's not that I don't like you," she continued, still struggling to resist the urge to knock the creature away. "Go on, go and cheer Parker up. She needs it more than I do. She'll certainly appreciate you a hell of a lot more."

Again she waited, but she was starting to feel more and more unhappy about the cat's presence. After a few more seconds, realizing that she could simply carry the animal across the landing and deliver it to Parker's room, she tried to sit up, only to discover that she was unable to move at all. She tried again, and although she could feel her muscles straining to move, she felt as if her bones were rigidly frozen in place, locked like lead pipes and somehow fused to the bed.

She instinctively tried to call out to Parker for help, but now she found that her jaw was just as immobile as the rest of her body. No matter how hard she tried to shout, all she could manage was the faintest murmur – a sound that had no hope of waking anyone.

Struggling again, she felt as if her bones weren't just frozen; they genuinely felt as if they'd been replaced by metal bars that were attached firmly to the bed, while her meat and flesh wriggled helplessly and hopelessly around those bars. She had no idea what could have caused such a thing to happen, but after a few seconds she fell still for a moment as she tried to come up with a better plan. A moment later, however, she felt a faint shifting of the bed, and she realized that the black cat had begun to make his way up past her waist.

Is this a stroke? she wondered. *Is those how it feels to die?*

Slowly the cat stepped into view, staring down at her with his two large yellow eyes. For her part, Alison could only try once again to move; her eyeballs at least were obeying commands, allowing her to look all around the room, but every other part of her body seemed frozen in place.

The cat continued to watch her, while regularly flicking his tail.

"Help me," Alison tried to say, even though all that emerged from her mouth was an unintelligible murmur. "Get help. Fetch Parker. Please, you have to help me, something's really wrong. I think it's sleep paralysis or something like that."

She waited, hoping against hope that somehow the cat might understand the problem, although deep down she knew she was clutching at straws. She tried again to sit up, and now her muscles felt so very tired as she strained them again and again against her unforgiving bones. For a few seconds she worried that she might actually rip her meat away from the bones beneath, but she still continued to strain until – utterly exhausted – she had no choice but to stop for a moment so she could try to gather her thoughts.

A few seconds later, the cat stepped even closer, until he was looking directly down into her eyes.

"You have to help me," Alison tried to say telepathically, even though she knew this approach had no chance of working. Then again, weren't cats supposed to be extremely sensitive? "I think I'm having a heart attack or something like that. Please, can you make a lot of noise? Can you find a way to wake Parker up? Knock something off the dresser! Make it smash! Isn't that what cats do all the time?"

Feeling increasingly frustrated, she stared back into the cat's calm eyes, and then she watched as the animal took a couple more steps forward, climbing onto her chest before stopping to once again look down at her face. Alison had never really been around pets very much, but she felt sure that they were able to sense when a human was in trouble; hadn't she read lots of stories in the news about cats and dogs saving the lives of their owners? Sure, she wasn't the cat's owner, but she felt that by now the wretched thing had to understand that something was really wrong.

Yet the animal merely stared and stared, before gently sitting on the lower end of her throat.

"Parker!" Alison tried to scream, once again hoping that she might eventually manage to force her mouth open. When that failed, she resorted to trying to groan as loudly as possible, but even this was clearly doomed.

And then, slowly, the cat reached forward with his right paw, moving the pads carefully toward Alison's left eye while gently tilting his head.

"What are you doing?" she tried to shout, still not managing to get any words out.

The paw stopped just an inch or two from Alison's eye. The cat seemed lost in thought, staring intently at the eye, until slowly five razor-sharp and very thin claws emerged silently from beneath the fur.

"What are you doing?" Alison tried again to ask, this time filled with fear, but her jaw remained locked in place.

In the darkness of the bedroom, moonlight

streaming through the window caught the cat's claws. Only able to move her eyeballs, Alison stared in horror as light glinted on the claws' curved edges and pinprick-sharp tips, but she told herself that the cat had no reason to hurt her; sure, she hadn't exactly welcomed the animal's arrival, and she'd heard that creatures could pick up on human vibes, but she reasoned that she'd still been fairly gracious. She certainly hadn't kicked the horrible thing or flung it out, so she tried to focus on the fact that she'd done absolutely nothing to make the cat in any way angry.

And then, slowly, the cat leaned forward until the tips of his claws were just millimeters from her left eyeball.

"Please," she tried to whimper, as she felt the first tear running down the side of her face, "don't do anything to me."

The cat stared at her for several more seconds, regarding her with the calm interest of a predator fully confident that its prey had been cornered, and then very slowly he tilted his paw and dipped the pads down, until finally one of the claws began to slice silently into the side of Alison's eyeball.

Feeling the pain but unable to scream, Alison could only whimper silently as the claw continued to cut carefully through the vitreous gel inside her eyeball. As well as the pain, she felt an anxious tugging sensation, and seconds later a series of black blotches began to fill her vision as the claw sliced up and out first through her pupil and then through the cornea, emerging with extra moisture added to its moonlit glint. The cat stared down at his work so far, before starting to gently lift his paw up, pulling on the front of Alison's eyeball as if trying to tear his claw straight through what remained of the cornea. When that failed to work, the animal tugged again, then again, as if trying to cause the maximum amount of damage with the least amount of effort.

As the pain intensified, and as the vision in her left eye faded to nothing, Alison couldn't even scream.

CHAPTER FOUR

UNTIL SUDDENLY SHE COULD.

Letting out a horrified cry, she sat up in bed, breathing big deep gulps and immediately reaching up to put a hand over her left eye. She could still feel the pain and the tugging sensation, and as she leaned forward she began to sob frantically. A few seconds later the lights in the room flickered on and she heard footsteps racing over to the bed.

"Mum?" Parker said frantically, sitting next to her. "What's wrong?"

"My eye!" Alison whimpered.

"What happened to it?"

"That cat!" Alison cried, using her remaining good eye to look around for a moment but failing to spot the animal anywhere. "It ripped out my eye!"

"Let me see."

"I need a doctor! You have to call an ambulance and get me to a hospital immediately!"

"Just let me see it first," Parker said firmly, before taking her mother's hand and gently moving it down from her face.

As soon as her eye was uncovered, Alison blinked and found that her vision had returned. She looked around, and her eyeballs – both entirely undamaged – darted first one way and then the other as they rolled perfectly normally in their sockets.

"I don't see anything wrong," Parker said, peering closer. "What exactly did the cat do?"

"It puts its claw in," Alison stammered, before crawling across the bed and then getting to her feet, hurrying to the dresser so that she could look in the mirror. "I couldn't move. It was like I was awake but I wasn't, and that awful cat sat on me and starting cutting my eye."

As soon as she saw her own reflection, she was relieved by the lack of obvious damage. She looked up and then down, then left to right, studying her eyeball intently; to her amazement, she saw only the usual slightly bloodshot veins that had emerged over a number of years, but the eye itself seemed to be entirely unharmed. She still couldn't help moving the eyeball around and around, convinced that at any moment she was about to spot the cuts caused by the cat's claw. The whole awful experience had felt so horribly real.

"You had a waking dream," Parker told her.

"A what?"

"Sleep paralysis. Whatever. You must have heard of it."

"I most certainly was not dreaming!" Alison barked, turning to her daughter. "What are you talking about? I know when I'm asleep and when I'm awake!"

"Your eye's fine," Parker pointed out, sounding a little weary now, "and in case you haven't noticed, there's no sign of the cat. It's not even in the house. I let it out earlier and it hasn't been back inside since, and as far as I know there aren't any hidden cat-flaps." She let out a heavy sigh. "This is perfectly understandable, Mum. You're stressed, you're in a new environment, and you've been through a lot lately. A little sleep paralysis is nothing to be ashamed of."

"It wasn't sleep paralysis!"

"Well, could you move?"

"No, but -"

"And despite apparently having the cat cut your eye, is your eye at all damaged?"

"No, but that doesn't -"

"I'd say that pretty much seals the case shut," Parker added confidently. She paused, before stepping over and placing her hands on the sides of her mother's arms. "Don't underestimate the immense pressure you've been under. If this is the only time the stress gets to you, then I'd take that as a big win. You've been so strong and brave, Mum, and it's only natural that eventually your brain fires off a few dodgy signals. Just be glad that it was a dream, and that you're fine." She paused. "I've probably made things worse. I'm sorry."

"The cat was in here," Alison replied meekly. "I saw it, and I felt it. I know you think I'm some weak-minded old fool, Parker, but I swear it was really here. It was on my bed!"

"I'll take a look around and double-check that it's out for the night," Parker replied. "Will that make you feel better?"

"It was so real," Alison told her, reaching up and touching the edge of her left eye again. "I really felt as if that claw was cutting into me."

"I've heard sleep paralysis can be like that," Parker said, before steering her back over toward the bed. "I know the whole process of buying this house was a nightmare, but now we're here and we can get on with sorting the place out. I'm sorry if I haven't been as supportive as I could have been, I'll try to do better. Now, if I go and check that there's no sign of the cat, do you think you can try to get some sleep?"

"Maybe," Alison said nervously, still looking around the room. "Just make sure that it's gone, okay? I can handle it being here during the day, but it's not to come into the house at night. Not ever!"

***

"Pussycat?" Parker said softly, keeping the lights off as she made her way barefoot across the hallway downstairs and into the front room. "Anyone here? Pussycat, if you're here, just let me know by meowing or something."

She stopped and listened, and a moment later she heard a door creaking open upstairs. She glanced over her shoulder, but to her relief she heard the bathroom light switching on, followed by a door bumping shut, and she realized that her mother was just making a little late-night visit to the toilet before trying to settle down again.

"Just like I told her," she continued, wandering across the front room and heading into the kitchen. "No sign of the -"

Suddenly she froze as she saw the cat sitting on the kitchen table, silhouetted against the moonlit window and purring as he stared back across the room.

"You nearly gave me a heart attack," she whispered, hurrying over. "How did you get back inside, anyway? Is this place full of holes?"

Stopping next to the table, she reached out

and stroked the back of the cat's head; letting out a continued low purring sound, the cat leaned toward her a little as if to let her know that he was perfectly happy with the arrangement.

"Listen," Parker said, "I know you didn't do anything wrong tonight, okay? But Mum... she's just very highly-strung and she gets these ideas stuck in her head, so you're going to have to go outside until morning. I think it's okay for you to come round during the day, I can even try to find some food for you, but at night you're gonna have to make other arrangements. That seems fair, doesn't it?"

Hearing the toilet flushing upstairs, Parker gathered the still-purring cat up into her arms and carried him over to the back door.

"Mum definitely can't know that you were in here tonight," she added, carefully unlocking the door and pulling it open, then setting the cat down on the back step outside. "She'd only freak out, and believe me, when she freaks out she *really* freaks out. It can last for days. She gets into one of her worry-holes and it's so hard for her to climb out again. So can you do me a favor? Can you find somewhere else to hang out at night?"

She watched as the cat walked slowly down the steps with his tail trailing behind; the tip briefly flicked.

"Mum had a weird dream about you cutting her eye open or something, and now she's kinda freaked out. So can we compromise?"

Reaching the bottom of the steps, the cat turned and looked over his shoulder. For a few seconds Parker felt as if the cat's eyes were burning into her, as if the creature was watching her intently, and she couldn't shake the sense that some powerful intelligence lay behind those eyes. She told herself that she was reading too much into the situation, but as she waited for the cat to walk away she began to feel a little guilty. After all, the animal possibly had nowhere else to go, and she desperately wanted to look after him properly; she knew her mother would never condone such an action, but she was already trying to think of ways to make the cat's life a little easier. She hated the thought that the poor thing had basically been turfed out of its own home.

"Parker?" Alison called out from upstairs. "Are you still down there? Did you find that cat?"

"No!" Parker yelled back at her, while keeping her eyes fixed on the animal and briefly raising a shushing finger to her lips. "Go to bed, Mum! I'll be up in a minute!"

She heard her mother's bedroom door bump shut, and for a moment longer Parker merely watched the cat as if the pair of them each wanted the other to break away first. Parker briefly felt as if she'd accidentally become a participant in some kind of primal game designed to establish dominance, although she quickly told herself that she was in danger of letting her imagination run wild.

"Make sure you come back tomorrow," she told the cat finally, before shutting the back door. "I'll try to find something for you."

CHAPTER FIVE

MORNING LIGHT STREAMED DOWN, breaking through the treetops and casting gently swaying summer shadows across the overgrown lawn. Somewhere in the distance, birds could be heard singing in the sunshine.

"This is definitely not going to cut it," Parker muttered as she sat cross-legged on the grass, examining the extremely rusted blades of a manual lawnmower she'd found under a pile of overgrown weeds. She was no expert, but the machine seemed to be absolutely ancient. "Mum!" she shouted. "It's no use, this thing's beyond repair! We're going to have to buy one!"

"Nothing's *beyond* repair!" Alison called back to her. "Put it to one side and I'll take a look. Even if it's no use as a lawnmower, I'm sure I can find another purpose for it."

"Maybe you can," Parker said, getting to her feet and carrying the old lawnmower over to the garage, "and maybe you can't, but that doesn't change the fact that you're gonna have to shell out for a new one."

She propped the lawnmower against the side of the garage, and then she turned to look out at the vastly overgrown grass at the far end of the garden. Someone had evidently done a little mowing at some point, probably just to make the house look presentable for prospective buyers, but that didn't change the fact that for the most part the grounds of the property were in a terrible state. Making her way over to the edge of the long grass, Parker realized that although there was something to be said for re-wilding the garden, her mother's boutique hotel plans were going to demand a more prim and proper appearance.

And that, in turn, meant getting a functional lawnmower.

"Parker?" Alison yelled. "Can you come up and give me a hand with this dresser?"

"On my way!" Parker called out, turning to head back inside, only to stop as she felt her left foot bump against something hard on the ground.

Looking down, she saw what appeared to be a chunk of old stone poking out from the beneath the dirt. She got down onto her knees and moved some of the grass aside, and sure enough she found herself peering at a roughly triangular chunk of gray stone, about ten inches tall at its tip and covered in yellowy-green moss. Evidently the stone had been in place for some time, and when she touched the broken edges Parker realized that they were fairly smooth, suggesting that they'd been worn down by many years of exposure to the elements. She gave the stone a tug, only to find that it was securely rooted in the ground, and then when she touched one side she felt a series of shallow grooves and indentations, almost like letters on the front of a gravestone.

"Weird," she muttered under her breath, unable to take her gaze off the stone for a moment. She paused, before slowly nodding. "Cool."

***

"A gravestone?" Alison said incredulously, as she finished propping a mirror on top of the dresser in one of the spare bedrooms. "Here?"

"Well, I don't know for sure," Parker replied. "I mean, that's definitely what it looked like, but there wasn't enough of it to be sure. Do you have any idea why there'd be a gravestone on the property?"

"Of course I don't!" Alison protested, as if she felt personally offended by the suggestion. "Are you out of your mind? People don't just go around burying other people willy-nilly all over the place like that, there are certain rules that have to be followed. For one thing, in case you hadn't noticed, this house isn't a church and the ground out there most certainly isn't consecrated."

"I know, but -"

"It's probably just a post."

"With writing on it?"

"Or a mile marker," Alison continued. "Did you work out what it said?"

"I couldn't," she explained, sounding a little frustrated now.

"I really need you to stay focused," Alison muttered, adjusting the mirror slightly in one direction and then in the other, as if a few centimeters either way would make the world of difference. "I get that you're not used to this sort of milieu, but that doesn't mean you have to go around inventing things."

"Milieu?"

"It means -"

"I know what it means, Mum," Parker said, and now her frustration was once again threatening to boil over. "Look, it's none of my business, anyway. It's your house and if there's a grave on it but you don't care, that's totally fine by me."

"There's not a grave on it," Alison replied through gritted teeth, peering at the mirror for a moment longer before reaching up and casually scratching at the edge of her left eye. "Now, come and tell me what you think of this. It's a beautiful old antique mirror but I'm really not sure that it belongs in this room. I'm getting so utterly stressed by the whole job and I think I'm losing my ability to remain objective. I want to try it in each bedroom, but somehow I keep getting distracted."

Stepping over to her mother's side, Parker took a moment to observe the mirror.

"It's fine."

"Fine?"

"It's fine," she said again, with a shrug this time.

"Fine's not enough," Alison said, heading to the dresser and lifting the mirror off. "You should know that by now. *Fine* doesn't cut it, not when you want to attract guests from London. These people expect everything to be perfect."

"Whatever," Parker said, rolling her eyes.

"Have you been to the village yet?"

"No," Parker replied. "Why would I have done that?"

"I asked you to go to the village and pick up the things I wrote on the list."

"You didn't mention any list," Parker said, following her mother through to one of the other bedrooms, where she saw her adjusting another mirror on top of a chest of drawers. "You know you're losing your memory, right? You never mentioned a list and you never asked me to go into the village."

"I most certainly did," Alison said firmly. "The list's on the side in the kitchen, so would you mind taking my bike and going to the local shop? My card's in my bag, and you know my pin number. I'm not even sure what the shops are like round here, but hopefully they stretch to a few of the basics, otherwise I'm going to have to drive to one of those soul-destroying out-of-town supermarkets. Those places drain my energy so terribly."

"Yes, Mum," Parker replied, resisting the urge to make any kind of sarcastic comment.

Hearing a rattling sound, she looked back out toward the landing. The sound had already stopped, but Parker was sure that for a fraction of a second she'd heard something metallic shaking, almost like... chains.

She began to count the bedroom doors.

"I'm convinced that supermarkets represent the decline of modern civilization," Alison continued, tilting her head as she assessed the mirror's position. "There's something so wretchedly awful about the convenience of all that tat and rubbish existing under one roof. I really don't believe that humans are designed to set foot in such places, and I'm sure real damage is caused whenever we do. I often think that I should refuse to ever go to one again, but then I remember that I too am just another weak individual with needs and wants. Then again, that's the sort of thing one should drum out of one's character, don't you think?"

She turned to Parker.

"No?"

"Sure, Mum," Parker said, turning and heading across the landing. "I'll just pop down to the local village, wherever that turns out to be, and see if they've got frozen pizzas and bottles of cola, because those are the things that are really going to save our souls."

"Don't be like that with me," Alison called after her, as Parker began to make her way downstairs. "Oh, and if you see the box with my healing crystals, can you bring it up here? I haven't done a session since we arrived and I'm already feeling dreadfully anxious and lethargic. I think that might be why I'm having so much trouble with these ruddy mirrors, it's almost like they're taunting me with their refusal to fit anywhere. I don't mind telling you that I'm already struggling a great deal with the energy flow of this house. I thought it'd be much easier to keep in order but it's utterly chaotic."

She looked around at the bedroom doors.

"Right," she continued after a moment. "Let's start again."

***

As she reached the kitchen, Parker could hear her mother still rambling away upstairs. Finding a list on the counter, she picked it up and glanced at the various items, and she felt her heart sink as she realized that this was going to be her life now; serving as an unpaid assistant for her mother's grand schemes wasn't exactly the exciting career she'd dreamed of, although she knew deep down that she was lucky to have a roof over her head and that plenty of people would kill for her opportunities.

"Back soon," she muttered, turning and heading to the door while her mother continued to talk to herself upstairs. "Don't do anything I wouldn't do."

CHAPTER SIX

"MAKE EVERY NIGHT A cocktail night," Parker read from the noticeboard outside the village pub, as she wandered back toward her bike with a couple of shopping bags. "I should be so lucky."

Once she'd set the bags on the handlebars, she began to turn the bike around ready for the ride home. After a moment, however, she spotted a sign on the front of a nearby building, and she slowed her pace before stopping to look at the open door.

"Local history hub?" she said with a faint smile. "How could a girl *not* be seduced by such a fascinating subject?"

As those words left her lips, she spotted a rather handsome dark-haired guy – roughly her age, and certainly her type – making his way over to the door and taping up a poster. The bundle of what appeared to be yet more posters and leaflets tucked under his arm suggested that he might have some connection to this history hub place. As the door swung shut, Parker realized that this was possibly the first sign of young life she'd seen in the entire area since arriving with her mother.

"Oh, go on, then," she said, propping her bike against a wall, then taking a moment to tie her hair back before heading over to the door. "Might as well get involved in the local community."

***

"Yes, Mrs. Bassletwaite, I've actually made quite a bit of progress on that front," the guy at the desk said over a cellphone, as Parker perused a set of nearby stands showing images of the village's history. "I've managed to track down your great-grandfather's work record, so I'm going to email that over to you right now."

Glancing at the guy, Parker was struck once again by his overall hotness, and by the fact that he seemed to have a brain as well. Keen to avoid getting caught staring, however, she returned her attention to the display while making sure to eavesdrop as much as possible on the conversation.

"In that case," the guy added after a moment, "I could drop over a thumb drive with all the files on. Would that be easier? I know the internet can be confusing. Do you know how to work a thumb drive?"

As the guy continued his conversation, Parker wandered over to another display, where she saw a poster advertising something called the Almsford Historical Reenactment Society. Almsford was a village not too far away, she was pretty sure of that, and according to the poster they had a penchant for reenacting key moments from their history.

"How utterly fascinating," she whispered, before looking at another display board and – to her surprise – spotting an old photo of Styre House.

"Excellent," the guy said over at the counter. "I'll pop that by this afternoon. I think you're really going to enjoy reading about your great-grandfather Eric. He led quite an interesting life, even if he hopped around a little from one job to the next. I'll have the drive to you by three."

Realizing that the call was over, Parker told herself not to rush over too quickly. After all, she really didn't want to seem eager, and she supposed that in fact she should probably wait and hope that he made the first move. She looked at some more photos of the house, partly because she was genuinely interested and partly because she was hoping to attract a little attention, and she figured that he'd have to talk to her eventually, especially since they were the only two people in the rather dusty and fusty-smelling room.

"Styre House," he said suddenly.

Startled, Parker turned to see the guy standing right behind her.

"In those photos," he continued, nodding at the pictures. "Sorry, I saw you looking so I thought I'd come over and see if I can help with anything. As it happens, Styre House is a subject of particular interest for me. It sold recently, I believe."

"I know," she replied, trying not to blush. "My mum bought it."

"She did?" Clearly genuinely enthused, he reached out and shook her hand. "That's wonderful. Sorry, I'm Colin, I kind of run the history hub single-handedly. Well, not single-handedly. Henry helps. Oh, but I suppose you don't even know who Henry is, do you? Sorry, am I rambling?"

"You must really love history," she said, although she immediately winced inside as she realized how banal she sounded. "To do it as a job, I mean."

"It's been a passion of mine for as long as I can remember," he replied, stepping to her side and looking more closely at the pictures on the display board. "Without local history, how can we understand our communities? Not everything has to be about the big, world-shaping events. Sometimes the really interesting stuff happens much closer to home."

"Totally," she replied, once again aware that she needed to say something a little deeper and more insightful, and preferably something funny too. "I'm Parker, by the way."

"You've moved into a fascinating place, Parker," he continued. "Styre House has always been one of the most interesting sites in the area. It's very old but the original parts of the building, as far as I'm aware, are in excellent condition. There's been some restoration work, of course, but it's all been very tastefully done and I'd say that the whole thing has been extremely respectful. Do you and your mother have any particular plans?"

"Mum wants to turn it into a hotel," Parker explained. "Or a holistic getaway for stressed-out executives. Or a kind of spa. To be honest, her plan changes pretty much every day, but the gist is that she wants to get rich people to pay to stay there." She looked at another of the photos. "Whether that plan works or not is -"

Before she could finish, she spotted a black cat in the image.

"Huh," she whispered.

"That's Smythe," Colin told her.

"I'm sorry?"

"It's just a little local joke," he continued with a smile. "The house has been empty for long periods, and naturally local children have loved going out there to scare themselves. A few rather foolish ghost stories have sprung up, but the most common one concerns that little fellow." He reached out and tapped the photo, just below the picture of the cat. "If you believe the stories, Styre House is haunted by the ghost of a black cat named Smythe who died many years ago. More than a century back, in fact."

"Is that so?" she replied, not really sure what she was supposed to do with that information.

"The legend goes that anyone who encounters Smythe is in for some serious bad luck," he explained. "There are so many different versions of the story, it's really hard to keep track. The most common version involves him guarding the property, waiting endlessly for his former owner. He doesn't take kindly to trespassers, either. He has a tendency to chase them away, as if he still believes that his long-dead owner is going to return one day and take the place on again."

"He sounds like a very loyal pet," she suggested.

"Obviously this photo shows an actual cat who must have lived there once," he pointed out. "There are a few others from over the years showing a similar cat, although obviously it can't be the same one. It's funny how local legends develop, though, isn't it? Someone probably saw a few of these pictures and spotted the cat, and then the whole story just ballooned out of control. Then again, my cynicism might be misplaced. What if there really *is* a ghostly black cat living out at the house? You should be careful, just in case he shows up."

"Totally," she replied, resisting the urge to mention the black cat she'd already encountered. After all, the last thing she wanted to do was make herself seem like an idiot. "I've got to admit, it's a pretty strange place. It has a real atmosphere." She paused, trying to think of some way to make him like her a little more. "Actually," she added, "I think I might have found a grave on the property."

"A grave?"

"Some kind of stone, at least," she continued. "Mum thinks it's just a marker, but I'm not so sure. It's definitely very old, but most of it must have been destroyed over the years. I think there was some text on it once, long ago, but that's been worn away."

"Fascinating," he replied. "I've certainly never heard of anything like that out at Styre House."

"You should come and see it!" she blurted out, before she had a chance to stop herself. "I mean, if you want to. Not if you don't. It's a free country, right?"

"I'd love to come and see the place again," he told her. "I've haven't been out there for many years, and I've never really had a chance to look around properly. I know I could have poked about, but it's private property and I never wanted to trespass. I've always been a bit of a stickler for the rules."

"Me too," she lied, while nodding sagely. "Me too."

Hearing the door creaking open, they both turned to see an elderly woman shuffling into the room.

"That's Mrs. Cricket," Colin said, lowering his voice a little. "She's something of a local legend, as it happens. It's best not to get on the wrong side of her, so I'd better go and see what she wants, but when's a good time for me to come and see the house? Would tomorrow be okay?"

"Tomorrow would be groovy," she replied, forcing a smile. "Really groovy. Just pop by whenever you can, I'm pretty sure I'll have been set to work on one job or another, but I can always take a quick break."

As Colin began to talk to the new arrival, Parker turned and looked for a moment longer at the photo showing the black cat. The animal looked *exactly* like the one that had made its presence known at the house, even if she knew that it couldn't possibly be the same cat; at most, there might be some kind of distant familial link, and as she made her way out of the hub she couldn't help wondering whether she should have mentioned the cat after all, if only to make herself seem a little more interesting. By the time she reached her bike outside, however, she had a far more pressing – and depressing – matter on her mind.

"Groovy?" she muttered under her breath. "Who says groovy? Why did *I* say groovy? Why can't I just act normal around a guy for once?"

AMY CROSS

CHAPTER SEVEN

"DISGUSTING THINGS," ALISON MUTTERED, visibly horrified as she held up a piece of rotten wood and stared at the silverfish scuttling about in a panic. Or whatever passed for panic in the silverfish world, at least. "As far as I can tell, this entire counter-top is riddle with them."

"How much of a problem is it?" Parker asked, standing next to her in the kitchen. "Do we need to pull it all out and start again?"

"That's about how it looks," Alison replied. "If -"

Suddenly the black cat jumped up onto the counter next to her, causing her to let out a shocked gasp as she pulled back.

"That damn animal!" she hissed, stepping away from the cat. "I really don't like it, Parker.

You're not encouraging it to come inside, are you?"

"Of course not," Parker replied with a grin, stepping over to the cat and stroking his back as he began to purr. "I think he just likes hanging out with us. Apparently there's a bit of a tradition of black cats in this house. In fact, there are even some pretty spooky stories about them."

"That's really not something I care to hear about," Alison said firmly. "You know, once we get this place up and running, that cat can't be in here. It's terribly unsanitary to have some kind of animal on the surfaces, and the guests won't like it."

"What guests?"

"I beg your pardon?"

"I know you don't like him, Mum," Parker said with a sigh, "but can't you at least give him a chance? Does he seem like some kind of awful monster to you?" Running a hand up the cat's back, she was surprised to feel some kind of old leather collar around his neck. "Besides, he probably belongs to someone who lives nearby. He's probably just trying to pull a fast one on us and get second dinners."

"I suppose he's not *that* bad," Alison muttered, before reaching out and running a finger against the side of the cat's face. "He seems healthy, at least."

"I think there's a tag on here," Parker continued, as she began to turn the collar around to get a better look. "It's almost -"

Suddenly the cat let out an angry snarl and swiped at Alison with his left paw, scratching her hand and drawing blood.

"What did you do?" Parker asked.

"Nothing!" Alison hissed, looking at the cuts on her hand before pushing the cat away, sending it leaping off the counter. "I just touched it, that's all!"

"You must have done *something*, Mum," Parker continued. "He wouldn't have just lashed out at you for no reason." She headed over to the cat, which had slunk away toward the back door. "Hey, little guy," she said, crouching down and trying again to look at his collar. "Mum's a good person, you don't need to be scared of her. Now, do you mind if I take a look at your collar? It feels pretty old and -"

Before she could finish, the cat pulled away again, keeping himself just out of reach.

"That thing's a menace!" Alison complained, heading to the sink and starting to run her hand under a cold tap. "I was just trying to be nice, and it attacked me!"

"You don't want to be touched, do you?" Parker said, watching as the cat backed away further into the corner. "You didn't mind it earlier, but... is it something about your collar? Is there some reason why you don't want me to touch that raggedy old thing?"

The cat turned and began to claw at the door. Realizing that he wanted to go outside, Parker got to her feet and turned the handle, and the cat immediately shot outside as soon as the gap was large enough.

"Poor little thing," Parker muttered. "He must be so scared."

"Oh sure," Alison replied, still holding her hand under the water, "by all means feel sorry for the cat. Meanwhile I'll just stand here and bleed to death!"

***

"So who are you going to vote for?" Parker asked that evening as she lay on the sofa, holding her phone and watching the television at the same time. "I'm totally going to pick Patrick and Lisa."

"Patrick and Lisa?" Alison replied, turning to her with a shocked expression. "Are you crazy? If anyone should be dumped, it's Eugene and Victoria!"

"I thought you liked Eugene when he was coupled up with Hoda?"

"That was a whole week ago," Alison pointed out. "A lot has changed since then. First there was the hot-tub incident, then he kissed that awful Meera woman and then at the last dumping -"

Before she could finish, they both heard a scratching sound coming from the back door. As voices continued to chat excitedly on the television, Parker and her mother looked over at the door, but with darkness outside they were only able to see a reflection of the living room.

"Did you hear that?" Alison asked.

"Hold on," Parker replied, getting to her feet. "Pause the show."

Reaching for the remote, Alison paused the episode.

"There's something out there," Parker continued, approaching the door cautiously as she heard the scratching sound again. "Wait, I think it might be the cat trying to get inside."

"Oh, don't let it in," Alison sighed. "It's feral! I've been saying that since the very beginning!"

"He's not feral," Parker said, stopping at the door and looking through the glass, finally spotting the black cat on the step. "Yeah, it's him," she added, unlocking the door before swinging it open. "I think -"

As soon as he had a chance, the cat darted through the gap, racing into the living room and then slowing as he approached the second sofa, where Alison stared back down at the animal with a troubled expression.

"It's looking at me, Parker," she complained.

"Why is it looking at me?"

"Have you considered the possibility that he likes you?"

"The feeling's not mutual," Alison grumbled. "Not remotely. And it's a -"

Stopping suddenly, she stared in horror at the cat.

"Parker, what's it doing now?"

"I'm sure he's fine," she replied, locking the door and then making her way back over. "And he's a 'he', by the way, not an 'it'. He's only -"

Before she could finish, the cat began to retch. Stepping to one side, Parker looked down just in time to see the cat leaning forward and extending his neck. Although she wanted to reassure her mother that nothing was wrong, she couldn't quite bring herself to say the words, and a moment later the cat suddenly jumped up and landed on Alison's lap, before swiftly vomiting up a small blob covered in a mix of saliva and blood.

"What's that?" Alison shouted, pulling back toward the other end of the sofa in a huge panic, sending the cat leaping back down and the blob falling to the floor. "Parker, what is it? What did it just do?"

"He threw up," Parker said, scrunching her nose slightly as the cat turned and walked away. "Gross."

"It did that on purpose!" Alison yelled.

"Look at it! It's proud of itself!"

"What is it?" Parker whispered, kneeling on the rug and leaning closer to examine the strange item. "It's really kinda solid, it almost looks like..."

She tilted her head a little to one side, and then she winced as she saw what appeared to be a small head.

"It's a mouse," she said finally, pulling back a little. "It's a dead mouse."

"Why did it do that to me?" Alison shrieked. "Why did it jump onto me and vomit a dead mouse?" She looked down at the front of her shirt. "It's left a stain! Parker, I've got cat vomit splattered on me, and blood from a dead mouse. Why would that horrible little monster do something like this?"

"Relax, Mum," Parker said, before grabbing a dirty plate and carefully using it to scoop up the corpse. "It's not *that* bad. Besides, it's probably a term of endearment in the cat world. It's like he's bringing you an offering in an attempt to make friends. You know, it's possible that this means he sees you as a kind of god."

"I don't want to make friends with it," Alison said, pulling her shirt off and holding it up so she could see the stain again. "And I don't want to be anyone's god. Oh Parker, I bet this won't even wash out. On my favorite shirt as well!"

Over by the door, the cat let out a loud meow.

"Now it's mocking me!" Alison wailed. "Did you hear that? It's celebrating its vindictive little victory!"

"Did you have to do this right now?" Parker asked the cat as she opened the back door again. The animal zoomed out and ran off into the night, and Parker took a moment to tip the dead mouse into a nearby bush. "You're not really helping much, not if you want Mum to like you."

"Horrible, wretched little monstrosity," Alison muttered, heading through to the laundry room. "I'm going to have to wash this on a high heat. It'll probably ruin the fabric completely."

"Nice peace offering," Parker said, rolling her eyes as she shut the door and turned the key in the lock. "Something tells me we're not going to be getting a pet after all."

CHAPTER EIGHT

"THIS IS A GRAVE," Colin said the following morning, as Parker held the long grass away from the broken stone in the garden. "It's *definitely* a grave, but..."

"But what?" Parker asked.

She'd intended to wait a few more seconds, to allow him to seem mysterious, but instead she'd been unable to help herself. She really wanted to know what was going on.

"This is going to sound really bad," he continued, "but while the house was abandoned and empty, I sort of... came snooping."

"You did, huh?" she replied, raising an amused – and ever-so-slightly impressed – eyebrow. "I thought you specifically said you *didn't* do anything like that..."

"I was... fudging the truth," he admitted. "I'm sorry, I just didn't know whether you'd get angry."

"Why would I get angry?" she asked. "I think it's kinda hot when someone breaks the rules. Kinda edgy."

"And I know it's possible that I missed something," he added, seemingly oblivious to her attempt at flirting as he pulled his phone out, "but I was pretty thorough. I didn't go into the house, because that would have meant breaking a window and I'm not that crazy, but I checked out the garden quite extensively." He tapped a few times, bringing up various photos before hesitating and then showing one to Parker. "There," he said. "See? One of the photos shows this exact spot, and there's no stone there."

"So what are you saying?" she asked. "Do you think someone put it in recently?"

"I don't know," he muttered, reaching over and tugging on the stone, only to find that it was held firmly in place. "It doesn't feel new."

"What if the grass was just covering it differently?"

"That doesn't explain the fact that it's not on *any* of the shots," he told her. "Besides, I hate to admit this but I can be rather anal about stuff like this. If there'd been a stone here, even the slightest hint of one, I'd have noticed. I swear."

"I believe you."

She waited for him to continue, but he was clearly utterly focused on the mysterious chunk of stone.

"What's the alternative, then?" she asked. "Are you saying that it... rose up from beneath the soil?"

Again she waited for an answer, but after a few seconds she began to wonder whether that might be exactly what he was suggesting.

"Wouldn't that be literally impossible?" she asked.

"Nothing's *impossible*," he replied. "There are just... different orders of likelihood."

"I don't think I'm smart enough to understand what you mean," she told him, "but I'm pretty sure gravestones don't just burst up out of the ground like this. Wouldn't that require a lot of force?" She looked at the stone again. "Wait, does this mean there might actually be someone buried in our garden? Like, an actual dead body? Is that what you're telling me?"

"I'm telling you that this house has a lot of history," he said darkly. "As it happens, last night I dug some more items out from my files. When I show you the photos, I think you're going to find them pretty interesting."

***

"Okay, there it is again," she said as they sat at the kitchen table, with mid-morning light streaming through the window and catching one of her mother's many glass ornaments, "but what exactly do you think it means?"

"Look at this one," he continued, sliding another photo across the table.

"Yes, I see it," she sighed, looking at the image of the house and seeing – yet again – that there was a black cat sitting on the steps at the back, "but why are you so bothered by this?"

"These two photos were taken fifty years apart."

"Black cats aren't that uncommon."

"They're wearing the exact same collar."

Peering at the two pictures, she saw that both black cats were wearing what appeared to be some kind of light collar with a small metal tag. The quality of the pictures wasn't good enough for her to make out any details, but she had to admit that there was a certain similarity.

"I was playing it cool yesterday," he told her.

"Could've fooled me."

"What?"

"Nothing," she replied, forcing a smile as she turned to him. "What do you mean?"

"I mean that I didn't want to freak you out at

the history hub," he continued, "but I think you need to know the truth. My interest in this house began as a simple historical exercise, but it soon developed to become much more than that. There have been rumors about the property for years, and they all circle back around to the same idea that it's haunted by a black cat."

Surprised by this suggestion, Parker could only stare at him with an expression of utter confusion. On the one hand she found Colin highly attractive, but on the other hand she was starting to think that he might be just slightly out of his mind.

"There's more," he added, pulling another set of files from his backpack.

"I'm sure," she muttered under her breath.

"In 1856, this house was owned by a woman named Lydia Smith," he explained, setting various photocopies of documents in front of her. "I don't know exactly where she came from, but people in the area soon began to whisper that she might have certain... abilities. There were rumors that she'd moved here after getting into trouble at home."

"What kind of trouble?"

"The kind where people die. I can't be sure, it's hard to separate fact from fiction in a lot of these cases. It's possible Lydia was the same Lydia Smith who was born not too far away in a village called Almsford. There are some really weird stories about that place. There's a legend about a woman called

Marston, but that's probably not strictly relevant in this situation. I've been meaning to do some more research into her, but when you get back that far the records are pretty patchy. Anyway, if we focus on Lydia for a while, some of the stories just got completely out of control."

"Oh great," Parker replied, "are we going to get into an actual witch-hunt now?"

"Lydia was shunned by the local community once she arrived," he continued, setting out some more documents. "No-one wanted anything to do with her. According to some of the stories, whenever she ventured into the village she was completely ignored, people simply acted as if they couldn't see or hear her. Eventually she stopped going at all."

"I'm not surprised if they were so rude," Parker told him.

"After that," he added, "the stories got wilder. By the late nineteenth century, no-one had seen Lydia Smith for years, and there were rumors that she might have died. If she was in her thirties in 1856, as the records seem to suggest, she would have been in her seventies by the turn of the century. The years are all kind of screwy, it's really hard to keep track. But then, one day, someone spotted her through a gap in the hedge and said she hadn't aged a single day."

"So it was her daughter."

"She didn't have a daughter."

"She had really good moisturizer."

He raised a skeptical eyebrow.

"Okay, so she was magic, then," she added with a hint of exasperation.

"You're not taking this seriously."

"I'm trying to," she complained, "but you're making it really hard. You're not even being consistent. One minute someone says she never aged, then in another story she's an old woman. Both those things can't be true."

She waited for an answer, but she was starting to think that she might have made her point pretty well.

"Aren't you supposed to be a local historian?" she asked, although she was keen to avoid sounding too harsh. "Don't you have a responsibility to stick to the facts, rather than encouraging people to spread scurrilous rumors? Surely a historian – of all people – should know the dangers of Chinese whispers and false claims about people being witches, right? This seems like the nineteenth century equivalent of fake news. Or are my standards too high?"

"So these stories spread and spread," Colin continued, as if he wanted to avoid directly addressing her question, "until they reached fever pitch. I've got hard proof that on the fifteenth of January in the year 1901, a meeting was held in the parish church. Concerned locals got together to discuss what to do about the evil on their doorstep."

"Evil?"

"They were worried," he explained. "A few weeks later, a local child went missing. A young girl named Verity Cain. She was never seen again, or one version of the story suggests that her body was found in the river, but I'm sure you can imagine that either way people were frantic. Eventually there was another meeting, in February 1901. By that point the locals must have been frantic. They genuinely believed that something evil and monstrous was in their midst."

"So what did they decide to do?"

"That's just it," he replied, "I have no idea. Whatever happened next was never written down. In fact, people seem to have gone to great lengths to avoid keeping any kind of record at all. But by the time of the next census just a few weeks later, this house was listed as unoccupied. In fact, the word 'unoccupied' was underlined several times as if someone wanted to emphasize that fact."

"They drove her out?"

"Or worse," he suggested. "Potentially far worse. If they'd merely driven her out, I imagine there'd be more mention of that fact in the records. They'd probably even have shouted it far and wide. Instead they seemed almost ashamed of whatever had happened, and I don't think it's too difficult to believe that something bad might have happened. Something *really* bad."

"Burn the witch!" Parker joked.

She waited for him to laugh, before realizing after a few seconds that he was serious.

"Here?" she said, barely able to stifle a chuckle. "In this sleepy little place? You're having a laugh, right? People here aren't a bunch of murderous psychos. Sure, back in the fifteenth or sixteenth centuries I'm sure witches were burned all the time, but that wouldn't have happened as recently as 1901."

"The house remained mostly empty for more than a century after Lydia Smith's disappearance," he replied. "There was a brief attempt to turn it into a boarding house, in circumstances that I don't quite understand, but that didn't last for long and then it lay empty again. Until it was finally purchased by your mother."

"And how does the cat fit in?" she asked, trying to seem untroubled by his claims. "What was his name again? Smithy? Smokey?"

"Smythe," he reminded her, "and if the stories are to be believed, he was Lydia Smith's companion. People have reported spotting him over the years since she disappeared. Just a few little claims here and there. The last one I managed to find comes from the late 1970s, when a cyclist late at night reported being followed by a black cat when he went past the house. He said it stuck with him almost until he reached the village, only to turn back once the lights of the local pub were in sight."

"Right," she said, feeling a shudder run through her bones.

"Have *you* seen a black cat here since you moved in?" he asked.

"Me?" She paused, wondering whether to add fuel to the fire of his conspiracy theories, or whether to take a respectful and careful step back. "Nope," she said finally. "Of course not. There's no freaky ghost cat here!"

CHAPTER NINE

"WHY ARE THE HOT ones always insane?" Parker asked, watching through the front window as Colin cycled away along the main road. "Or is it that the insane ones are always hot? And if that's true, then what does it say about me? Am I a freak?"

She waited until he was out of sight, and then she turned to see that her mother hadn't been listening to a word she'd just said. Instead, Alison was sitting at the table and rubbing her left eye as if she was bothered by some kind of irritation.

"Mum?" she continued. "I just had my hopes and dreams of a steamy rural romance crushed, and you're not even paying attention! Do you think I'm ever going to find a nice, stable guy to go out with, or am I doomed to linger with the freaks and weirdos? And what does that say about me?"

"What was that?" Alison asked, still rubbing her eye furiously. "I'm sorry, I think I've got something in here, it's really irritating me."

"Let me take a look," Parker said, wandering over as Alison turned to her. "You probably just rubbed some paint-stripper or -"

Before she could finish, she saw that her mother's left eye was bloodied and slightly swollen. She tried not to show any disgust, but she couldn't help flinching as she saw the thick, over-sized veins that seemed to be almost running directly into the pupil.

"Be honest with me," Alison said, her voice tense with fear, "how bad does it look?"

"It could be worse," Parker suggested cautiously. "I mean, I'm not quite sure how, but..."

"I must be allergic to something," Alison continued, getting to her feet and heading to the sink. "It's been a little dry all morning, but in the last few minutes it's really been getting much worse. Do you think it's possible to be allergic to silverfish?"

"I'm not sure that's an allergy," Parker replied, unable to hide a growing sense of concern. "Mum, are you sure you shouldn't see a doctor?"

"Why? So I can be misdiagnosed and given some kind of drug that the big pharmaceutical companies are paying those quacks to dish out?"

She let out a derisory sniff as she ran some tap-water into the palm of her hand and then splashed her inflamed eye. "No way. Not me. I'll look online for some herbs that might help, and I'll light one of my healing candles. I'm sure that'll fix it. And I'm not going to look in any mirrors."

"You're not?"

"That only makes it worse," Alison said as she headed out of the room. "This is an old psychological trick I learned once from a teacher I met while I was traveling around India. If you look at an injury, you make it worse by imagining how it could develop. Whereas if you don't look at it, it heals unobserved and without causing any stress."

"That makes no sense," Parker replied, "but then again, that's just about par for the course round these parts. You do your thing, Mum, but I've got a feeling you're going to need to see someone about that eye pretty soon." She waited, but all she heard in response was the sound of her mother knocking over various items in the medicine cabinet above the sink in the downstairs bathroom. "It's fine," she added. "You can just die from some perfectly treatable eye infection and I'll be condemned to live all alone here for the rest of my life, unable to even attract the local nutters."

A floorboard creaked above her. Looking up, Parker briefly wondered which room the sound had come from, but she soon felt a flood of despair rushing through her body.

"I'm destined to die alone and miserable. Perhaps I'll become a crazy cat lady."

***

"I *would* date a lunatic," she continued half an hour later, still muttering away to herself – having never really stopped – as she leaned a selection of rusty garden tools against the side of the garage. "I'm not saying that it's my preference, but I'm not picky. I'd just like to feel wanted. And I could even visit him at the local asylum. Hell, at least I'd always know where to find him."

Hearing a rustling sound, she turned to see that the black cat had returned.

"Hey there," she said, before furrowing her brow as she realized that the cat was ignoring her. "Even *you* don't care, do you?"

The cat hopped up onto a bench and made his way to the other end, before jumping down over the other side.

"Hey!" Parker called out. "Are you not even going to look at me? Is this how you treat your new friends, Smythe?"

Suddenly the cat froze, and after a few seconds he slowly turned and looked directly at Parker. In that moment, staring back at the cat, Parker realized in turn that he was carrying something in his mouth. After glancing around for a few seconds, she began to make her way over to the animal, before crouching down so that she could see a little better.

"Another mouse, huh?" she said, spotting the carcass clenched between the cat's jaws. "Nice. I bet you get some good hunting round these parts, don't you?"

She waited, but now there was something slightly unnerving about the cat's incessant, determined glare.

"That was a pretty mean stunt you pulled last night," she added. "If you want to get fed any of that fancy cat food from the adverts, you're going to have to be nicer to Mum, okay? She controls the purse strings, and I sure as hell can't afford to buy you a load of food." She saw some glistening blood leaking out from the dead mouse. "Fresh kill?" she added with a sigh. "I guess you're not relying on us for food at all, are you? But I bet you like cuddles."

Again she waited, and again the cat merely stared back at her. After a few seconds, however, Parker spotted a glint of light reflected against the rusty old tag hanging from the creature's collar.

"Do you mind if I take a look at that?" she asked, before very slowly reaching closer. "I won't hurt you, I promise. I'm actually very friendly. I just want to see what it says on there, that's all."

Touching the tag, she immediately felt that

the metal was rough and damaged, as if it had been out in the elements for quite some time. She could just about feel a few indentations, however, suggesting that there might be some text on the collar after all.

"Let me just get a better look," she continued, leaning closer. "I'm not -"

Before she could finish, the cat turned and hurried away, expertly slipping across the garden before disappearing into a gap in the wall on the side of the old garage. Getting to her feet, Parker hurried over, but when she crouched down and peered through the gap she was unable to see whatever might be on the other side.

"Hello?" she called out. "Pussy? Smythe? Is that's your name? I just want to be your friend. There's no need to be so jumpy all the time."

She waited, but she heard no reply. Rolling her eyes, she stood again and walked around to the rear of the garage, only to find that the rickety old wooden door was securely locked. She hadn't actually managed to get a look inside the garage yet, and although she had no expectation that it might contain anything interesting, she couldn't help trying the door a couple more times.

"This thing's so old, a stiff breeze'd probably blow it over," she said under her breath. "Hey, Smythe, are you in there? Can you hear me?"

Silence.

"I get it, you know," she continued, with a hint of sadness in her voice. "You just want to be left alone, don't you? I bet this place was an absolute paradise for you before we showed up. I don't know where you came from, but you had the run of the house and the grounds, and I bet the day Mum and I arrived was the day your whole world changed."

Silence again.

"I know what it's like to have your whole world change overnight," she added softly. "To have it all come crashing down. Mum's great, she's kind and generous and adventurous and I love her so much. That's why I feel so guilty for missing Dad so much. I know she misses him too. When he died, I felt like nothing was ever going to be the same again, and do you know something?"

More silence.

"I was right," she said sadly. "Totally right. One hundred per cent on the money. Nothing *has* been the same, and it never will be. But we all have to make the best of the cards we're dealt, Smythe, so if you're unhappy about us being here... join the club. And maybe try to hang out with us some more, okay? Preferably without antagonizing Mum too much more. She's really not so bad, not once you get to know her. In fact, and it pains me to say this, she can actually be pretty damn cool."

She waited, not really expecting an answer

but wondering whether the black cat was listening to her from the other side of the door.

"Well," she muttered finally, "when you're ready to have your belly scratched, or chase a ball or whatever, you know where to find us. Just don't be a stranger. I've got a feeling we might actually become really good friends. If you give it a chance, at least. And I'm sorry, okay? For disturbing you. I'm really sorry if we showed up and ruined all your plans."

CHAPTER TEN

"DO YOU THINK I'D suit all black?" Parker asked that night, as she made her way up the stairs, heading for her bedroom. "I think I might become one of those people who wear all black, all the time. That'd warn people to stay away from me, right?"

Passing the door to her mother's room, she heard a few whispered mutterings. Parker was more than accustomed to talking to herself, and she knew her mother had a tendency to not bother listening, but after a moment she stopped and took a couple of steps back. Leaning past the open door, she saw to her surprise that Alison was sitting on the end of the double bed, seemingly engrossed by the sight of her own belly.

"Are you okay, Mum?"

Receiving no answer, she considered simply

going to bed, but finally she strolled into the room and made her way over to check that nothing was wrong. As she got closer, however, she saw that her mother was picking at a large scab of loose skin just to one side of her belly button, with raw and reddened patches showing through from underneath.

"What's going on there, Mum?" she asked, stopping in front of her and looking down at the patch. "Have you suddenly got eczema?"

"It's nothing," Alison murmured, as if she'd barely heard her daughter's voice at all. "I'm fine. Go to bed."

"Do you think it's another allergy?"

"I said it's nothing!" Alison hissed, still scratching at the wound.

"You probably shouldn't pick at it," Parker suggested. "It's not -"

"I said, go to bed!" Alison snapped, looking up at her, glaring with one normal eye and one that was swelling almost out of its socket. "Go to bed right now, and don't bother me!"

"Mum, what's going on with your eye?" Parker gasped. "Can you even see out of it right now? It looks really awful!"

"You don't know what you're talking about," Alison sneered, reaching up and wiping some clear liquid from the side of the socket. "Do you think I need your opinion right now, Parker? I'm more than capable of looking after myself, I've been all alone ever since your father died so there's no point in you suddenly acting like you care now! Just go to bed and leave me alone!"

"Mum, chill out!" Parker protested. "I was only -"

"Why won't you just leave me alone?"

Grabbing Parker by the shoulders, Alison manhandled her out of the room, shoving her onto the landing before slamming the door shut, sealing herself inside.

"Mum, calm down!" Parker said, shocked by everything that had just happened. "Have you completely lost your mind? I'm trying to help you!" She waited for an answer. "Mum, don't take this the wrong way," she continued, "but I'm worried about you."

"I probably just ate some gluten by accident," Alison replied from behind the door. "You know what it does to me."

"Gluten doesn't make your eye swell up!"

"It might if I haven't had it for a while. The human body adapts and adjusts, and then if you throw toxins back into it after a long period of cleansing, it has a tendency to... overreact." A bump rang out, followed by the sound of something falling from one of the cabinets. "The last thing I need is for you to make a fuss, Parker, so will you please just go to bed? I promise you, everything's going to be alright."

"I -"

Stopping herself just in time, Parker realized that there was absolutely no point arguing with her mother. Besides, things usually worked out, and she supposed that the swollen eye would most likely be fine in the morning; and if it wasn't, then her mother would just have to go to the doctor, because she obviously couldn't go around with one eyeball almost popping out.

"See you in the morning, Mum," she said wearily, as she turned and headed to her room. "Just... try not to have any more weird reactions to anything for a while, okay? Believe it or not, I actually worry about you."

***

An owl hooted in the distance, followed by the sound of a fox screaming, as Parker lay in bed and stared up at the shadows on the ceiling. Moonlight was casting strange shapes across the paint as trees blew in a gentle breeze outside; with the bedroom lights off, Parker had been hoping to get some sleep but instead she found herself wide awake as her mind filled with all sorts of crazy ideas.

Worst of all, she couldn't stop thinking about her mother's swollen eye. No matter how hard she tried to convince herself that she didn't need to worry, deep down she knew full well that something was very wrong.

Eyes just didn't do that sort of thing.

At least, not without causing serious long-term damage.

Suddenly feeling a bump on the bed, Parker began to sit up, only to see a dark shape moving across the other end of the duvet. For a fraction of a second she wondered what was happening, but at the last moment she saw the telltale flick of a cat's tail.

"Oh, it's you," she said with a faint smile, and sure enough she heard a purring sound as the cat began to make his way along the bed. "How do you keep getting in and out like this? Is there some secret hole that we know nothing about?"

Still purring as he reached the top of the bed, the cat began to lean against Parker, and in turn she reached out and began to stroke his side. A chain briefly rattled somewhere nearby, perhaps in the next room, but she barely noticed that sound at all as she focused entirely on the cat.

"You like me, do you?" she continued. "Well, I like you too, but you're gonna have to be nicer to Mum. I don't know what's going on with her eye, but she reacts badly to stress and I think maybe this whole move is getting to be too much for her. Either that or her blood pressure is so high now that bits of her body are literally popping out.

That actually doesn't seem completely impossible."

The cat turned around and pushed against her from the other side, before climbing onto her chest and stopping to look down at her.

"So now you're being all cute, are you?" Parker asked, before once again spotting the tag hanging from the cat's collar. "Obviously *someone* owns you," she pointed out, "or at least they did in the past. Would you mind terribly if I take a look and try to find out who? You didn't seem too keen last time, but I'm kinda curious. Then again, you know what they say. Curiosity killed the -"

She caught herself just in time.

"Well," she added hesitantly, "let's not think about that particular phrase."

She waited a few seconds longer, before very slowly reaching up and taking hold of the tag. To her surprise the cat seemed totally unbothered, so she tilted the tag so that she could try to see its surface in the moonlight, although she quickly found that any lettering – if there had ever been any at all – was clearly long gone; indeed, the tag itself seemed ancient, with battered edges, and Parker couldn't help but wonder whether it might even have been homemade. Still, something about the tag kept her attention, almost as if the small piece of metal was in some way familiar.

She didn't even notice as a chain rattled briefly on the other side of the wall.

"It's pretty," she said softly, before looking up into the cat's eyes. "You seem kinda healthy for a cat that's apparently living wild. I guess a diet of mice and other rodents must be doing wonders for you."

She began to stroke the cat's side, and she could feel his whole body vibrating slightly as his purrs continued. The tail flicked, and the cat seemed to be enjoying himself until – with no warning – he suddenly turned and looked over at the window. As the purring stopped abruptly, Parker waited to see what might be wrong, but a moment later the cat turned and raced back down the bed, jumping off the end and hurrying out of the room.

Sitting up, Parker listened to the sound of the cat rushing down the stairs, and then she clambered out of bed and headed to the window just in time to see the animal skulking out across the patio.

"You're a quick little thing, I'll give you that," she said, as she watched the cat examining one particular patch of grass. She quickly realized that this was where she'd found the piece of stone jutting out of the ground, the same piece that Colin had been so convinced must be part of a grave.

Parker, meanwhile, had begun to abandon that idea, figuring that there was simply no way there could actually be a grave on the property. Sure, the stone *looked* like part of a gravestone, but she couldn't quite bring herself to believe such a crazy idea.

A few seconds later the cat raced across the lawn and disappeared into the shadows that covered one end of the garage.

"Suit yourself," Parker said, wandering back over to the bed and flopping down, before pulling the duvet over herself. "You could sleep in here on a nice big soft bed, but I'm sure the garage is much nicer."

***

Outside, a mouse scurried through some long grass before stopping and sniffing the air. As if it had suddenly sensed another presence near the door to the garage, the mouse looked around, watching for any sign of movement. As it did so, it failed to notice a pair of yellow eyes moving closer from behind.

CHAPTER ELEVEN

"OKAY," ALISON SAID BRIGHTLY the following morning, turning away from the sink to see that Parker was sitting at the kitchen table, "let's hit the ground running and -"

"What the hell?" Parker gasped.

"Have you never seen an eye-patch before?" Alison sighed. "Please, Parker, I don't have time for more of this nonsense. I had one in my medicine box and I thought I'd wear it for a day or two, just until my eye calms down."

"It looks like something's bulging out from underneath!"

"Parker..."

"Have you taped it into place?"

"Parker, I won't tolerate this silliness," Alison continued, clearly determined to maintain a chipper mood. "Today we're going to be scraping the outside of the house. It's a long and boring job, there's no glory in it, but it's absolutely essential. Now, do you know why we're going to be scraping the house?"

"Because we're country people and this is what passes for entertainment around here?"

"Because we're getting ready to paint it," Alison explained as she took a seat. "I've got it all worked out, we need to scrape the old paint off before we can apply the nice new paint I've got coming at the weekend. I know this must seem like a dull and thankless task, but sometimes we have to do the boring work first and then all the fun stuff comes later. It's called delayed gratification. Do you know anything about that?"

She waited for a response.

"Parker? Do you know what delayed gratification is?"

"I'll tell you later," Parker replied. "What's going on with your skin?"

"My skin?"

"It looks kind of red," Parker continued, peering at her mother's neck, where puffy blotches had begun to develop, some with what appeared to be small boils starting to show through. "Do you think maybe you should see a dermatologist? Mum, no offense, but you're looking kind of... gross."

"Can we please stop with the amateur

medical examinations?" Alison asked, getting to her feet again. "I've got some scrapers outside and they should be fairly self-explanatory. Do I need to show you how to use them, or can I get on with some other work and leave you to do this under your own steam?"

"I'm sure I can figure out how to scrape," Parker told her. "I'm not a complete and utter moron."

"One would hope not," Alison said as she hurried out of the room, seemingly in something of a mild panic. "Let's see how today goes, shall we? I do hope I can start to rely on you a little more, Parker. I don't want to have to do *everything* myself."

***

"Styre House? What are you looking at that old place for?"

Having been engrossed in his research at the history hub, Colin hadn't even noticed that he had company. Now he watched as Henry Overton, the other regular volunteer, limped around to the other side of the table.

"Someone bought the place, Henry," he explained. "They just arrived the other day."

"Yes, I heard about that," Henry muttered, setting some books down. "Such a pity. I'd really hoped that it might stay off the market after the parish council managed to get ahold of it all those years ago, but eventually they insisted that they had to sell it to raise money after the latest round of budget cuts."

"How long had the parish council owned it?" Colin asked.

"A hundred years, maybe even more," Henry explained, with a hint of irritation in his voice. "I'm a little foggy on the details, but they were determined to just leave the place alone. I think they rather hoped that Mother Nature would take care of things and the house would rot and fall down. Lord knows, there have been some mighty storms over the years, but never enough to quite finish the wretched place off."

"So why sell it?"

"Money, I'm afraid," Henry said, heading to the sink and pouring some water into the kettle. "The library needs a new carpet. The defibrillator in the old phone box needs some new signs. Some local oik smashed the bus stop up and the glass needs replacing. All those things cost money, and money's one thing that the parish council's always short of. I mean, sure, they've got enough to send a bunch of bigwigs off for a twinning trip to France, wining and dining themselves and -"

"I know about your issues with the council," Colin replied, interrupting him. "I still don't quite get what any of that has to do with Styre House."

"I believe Styre House was at one point listed as an asset of community value," Henry explained. "Perhaps someone eventually forgot to do the paperwork and keep it that way. Or, more likely, it was just how I suggested and money was tight. The budget needed to be balanced so people started looking around for anything that could be flogged off. And I suppose the superstitions began to fade, like they always do. Suddenly Styre House didn't seem like such a big problem."

"In what way?"

"People used to be so afraid of that house," Henry continued, setting the kettle on to boil. "When I was a young lad, you could barely get anyone to even acknowledge that the place existed. I explicitly recall cycling past with my old mum one afternoon and asking her about it, I must've been only about ten years old, and she denied that there was even a house there. You could see a part of it poking out from behind the trees, but she swore blind that I was mistaken."

"That's crazy," Colin agreed.

"As I got older, I began to understand," Henry replied. "Superstitions are often superstitions for a reason, you see. They're a kind of collective memory, and the collective memory of this place wanted Styre House to be left completely alone. And that idea persisted for generations, not always sharp and in focus, but it persisted nonetheless and..." He paused, and then he let out a heavy sigh. "Eventually these things wear off. New people take over and they're less respectful of the old beliefs. They think they know better. To them, that patch of land would have seemed like nothing more than a local asset that could be sold off to plug a funding gap."

"That seems... short-sighted."

"Welcome to the real world," Henry muttered. "I'm sure the decision was made by the same out-of-touch idiots who had no problem letting the old pub on Carver Hill get knocked down a few years ago. They don't care about the local community. You have no idea how many backhanders get passed around in brown paper envelopes."

"I get it now," Colin told him. "Still, it seems a little odd that no-one thought to warn the new owners that the house has a... well, a kind of past."

"Why drive down the sale price when there's no need?" Henry pointed out as the kettle boiled next to him. "I'm sure the parish council think there's no harm in having people living out there again, and they might well be right."

"How much of the old legend about the place do you think is true?"

"All of it," Henry said, taking the two least

chipped mugs from the shelf and setting them down, then grabbing some teabags. "None of it. Some of it. Who knows? I certainly haven't heard any spooky claims about Styre House over the past few years. For all we know, the house might have... calmed down."

He set the teabags into the mugs, and then he looked once more at the papers Colin had been studying on the table.

"Why are you so interested?" he asked.

"I went out there yesterday," Colin explained. "I was invited by the girl who lives there with her mother. The strange thing is, I found something that might have been part of an old gravestone. I keep changing my mind about it, to be honest, but I can't shake the feeling that something isn't quite right." He hesitated as the kettle began to boil. "What do you think happened to that Lydia Smith woman?"

"The one from the 1900s?" Henry replied, and now he seemed noticeably less comfortable. "Who knows? I doubt it was anything too sinister. She probably just moved away."

"What about the black cat that's been seen up there?"

"Black cats are ten-a-penny round these parts," Henry pointed out as he began to pour boiling water into the mugs. "I wouldn't read too much into any of that nonsense." He set the kettle back down, and then he watched for a moment as Colin began sorting through some photocopies. "So tell me something," he added cautiously. "This girl who lives there with her mother... would she happen to be around your age?"

"Roughly," Colin replied absent-mindedly. "Maybe a year or two younger."

"And is she... a nice person?"

"Really nice."

"And is she easy on the eye?"

Colin looked up and glared at him.

"There's nothing wrong with that," Henry added, unable to stifle a grin. "The life of a historian can often be a lonely one. If you've found yourself a nice young lady to pursue then I wish you all the luck in the world. You never know, you might find that the way to her heart is through the deeds associated with her mother's new property."

"That sounds *very* romantic," Colin replied, rolling his eyes as he looked at the various photos again. "Not that I care about anything like that, of course."

"Of course."

"I'm solely interested in the history," he added, worrying that he might have started blushing. "When I was out there yesterday, I couldn't shake the feeling that something was wrong. Something I couldn't quite put my finger on." He looked at another photocopy and saw that this particular picture, like a number of the others, showed a black cat sitting near the property. "It's as if my intuition's playing up somehow, like some part of my subconscious mind has noticed a pattern and now it's trying to make my conscious mind sit up and take pay attention."

"Are you sure you're not reading too much into all of this?" Henry asked.

"I probably am, but I really need to study the place a little more," Colin muttered. "Sorry, I don't think I'll be much use for the rest of today. I'm too engrossed in this whole story."

"Yes, I can tell," Henry replied, as the smile began to fade from his face. He watched Colin working for a moment longer, before pulling his phone from his pocket and starting to surreptitiously type out a message. "I'm sure it'll be fine," he added, tapping to send the message and then seeing that the other person was already working on a reply. "Don't worry about anything else today. Just stay here and do some research. In fact, it's lucky that you're able to hold down the fort."

A reply appeared on the screen; after reading the curt two-line message, he slipped his phone away.

"Actually, Colin," he added, "if you don't mind, I just need to pop out for a few hours."

CHAPTER TWELVE

"SCRAPE SCRAPE SCRAPE," PARKER said, as she used the plastic device to chip away more loose paint from a patch high up on the house's south-facing wall, near her mother's bedroom window. "Scrape scrape scrape scrapity scrape scrape -"

Before she could finish she spotted movement out of the corner of her eye. Turning and looking down, she spotted the black cat making his way across the lawn with something in his mouth; she squinted, and she was just about able to make out what appeared to be yet another mouse carcass.

"Glad to see I'm not the only one being useful," she muttered under her breath before getting back to work, scraping some more paint away.

Stopping again, she looked along the side of

the house and saw another window. She furrowed her brow as she tried to work out what room that particular window looked into; she thought of the house's layout and the various bedrooms, yet somehow she wasn't quite able to get things straight in her head. The more she looked at that other window, the more she felt as if something wasn't right. She told herself that she'd have to move the ladder later and take a look into the next room along, but for now she decided to focus on the scraping at hand.

A couple of minutes later, spotting movement on the other side of the window in front of her, she looked into her mother's bedroom just in time to see the cat carrying the dead mouse toward the bed.

"Hey!" Parker hissed, waving frantically. "Don't do that! If she finds out, she'll kill you!"

The cat glanced at her but failed to break his stride as he ducked under the bed.

"No!" Parker sighed, tapping gently against the glass. "That's so not cool! Dude, you're really not helping yourself!"

A moment later the cat emerged, and Parker breathed a sigh of relief as she saw that he was still carrying the mouse, having evidently failed to deposit it under the bed.

"Get out of there!" she said, watching as the cat hurried out of the room. "Okay, that's better. If you really have to put it somewhere, just put it under *my* bed and I'll get rid of it later." She started scraping again. "Not that I particularly want to be gathering up corpses, but it's better than Mum losing her nut."

Spotting movement again, she watched as her mother stepped into the bedroom. Reaching out, Parker was about to tap on the window and wave, but she hesitated at the last second as she saw Alison approaching the mirror in the far corner; curious to see what her mother might be up to, she watched as Alison turned and lowered her gown, revealing a set of thick sores all over her back.

"What the hell?" Parker whispered as her mother, unaware she was being watched, turned her back to the mirror and looked over her shoulder, attempting to see the sores a little better.

Glancing down, Parker saw the black cat heading out of the house, still carrying the dead mouse as he headed over toward the garage.

"All human life is here," she sighed, before turning to see that her mother had pulled the robe back up and was walking over to the bed. After a couple of paces, however, Alison stopped and – finally realizing that she was being observed – stared at her daughter.

Who, in turn, waved.

"How's it going out there?" Alison shouted, clearly struggling a little to act as if nothing was wrong.

"Fine!" Parker called back to her. "It's a fascinating process. I mean, I used to think it was exciting to watch paint dry, but now I actually get to watch paint *stay* dry instead. I'm just worried I might pass out due to all the excitement and fall off the ladder!"

"I know!" Alison replied, without a hint of irony as she exited the room. "I'm so glad you feel that way! I'm always so fascinated by paint as it comes away. I might gather up the flakes from the grass below you and try to use them in my art."

"Yeah, you do that," Parker said, furrowing her brow before looking over at the garage.

This time, there was no sign of the black cat, and she could only assume that it must have gone into either the garage or one of the other outbuildings. A moment later she spotted something moving out on the road, but when she turned to look there was no sign of anyone. She waited, convinced that she'd seen a figure walking past, although after a few more seconds she realized that she must have been mistaken. For a fraction of a second she'd hoped that Colin might be about to make a reappearance.

"Don't lose your mind, Parker," she whispered, getting back to work as her mother appeared below and – true to her word – started gathering the pieces of dried paint from the grass.

"After all, you're pretty much the only one here who's got any sanity left at all."

***

Crouching down on the road, taking care to avoid being seen over the low hedge, Henry Overton hesitated for a few more seconds before daring to crane his neck again. He knew he'd almost been spotted once already, and he couldn't risk a repeat.

"Parker, have you seen my crystals?" a voice called out.

Henry stayed completely still, although he'd already spotted a gap in the hedge.

"I'm sure they're exactly where you left them, Mum!" another voice replied.

"Well, I can't find them at all," the first voice continued. "You must have moved them."

Henry heard the second voice muttering curses under its breath, and a few seconds later he craned his neck and peered into the garden, just in time to see that the girl had climbed down the ladder and was storming – unhappily, he could tell – into the house.

Realizing that this was his chance, Henry hurried to the gap in the hedge and began to squeeze through. He found that progress was harder than he'd expected, and he had to twist a few times in order to get free from branches that caught on his shirt, but finally he emerged at the side of the garage. After taking a moment to dust himself down, he made his way to the end of the structure and peered past the corner; he could just about hear voices shouting inside the house, accompanied by the distant sound of stomping feet, and he told himself that hopefully the house's inhabitants would be busy arguing for quite some time to come.

A moment later, spotting movement, he looked over his shoulder just in time to see a black cat carrying a dead mouse to a small hole at the bottom of the wall. The cat stopped for a moment and glanced at Henry, staring at him with what Henry felt was quite some degree of intelligence, and then the animal slipped quickly and gracefully through the hole, disappearing from sight.

"I recognize you," Henry muttered under his breath, before looking at the padlock on the garage's wooden door. "Perhaps we should start here."

Reaching into his pocket, he pulled out his portable toolkit – or 'Action Kit', as he preferred to call it – and took out one of the screwdrivers. While repeatedly looking over his shoulder to make sure that he wasn't about to be spotted, he worked to remove the bolt from the door, attempting to bypass the padlock entirely. He'd always been rather proud of this little trick, while wondering why other people so often failed to understand that the easiest way through any locked door was always to find the weakest connection, and after just a few more minutes he was able to pull the entire lock away. Grabbing the edge of the door, he carefully pulled it open until he was struck by a whiff of cold, damp air drifting out from the long-undisturbed garage.

Slipping inside, he took care to shut the door again before turning and looking along the dark, narrow space. He couldn't see much, although slivers of light were shining through dirty windows on one wall and some more light had managed to get through cracks in the wooden roof. So far, however, all Henry could make out was an unholy collection of boxes and other items that had seemingly been abandoned long ago.

Pulling out his phone, he typed out another quick message to the chairman of the historical society.

"Just having a poke around," he whispered, reading the text out loud. "Will report back later."

A few seconds later, however, he heard the tell-tale sound of something bumping against one of the boxes, and he realized that the cat was somewhere nearby.

"It's you, isn't it?" he said cautiously, taking a couple of steps forward. "The others told me I was crazy, but I've seen you in lots of those photos. You've been hiding in plain sight this whole time and -"

Suddenly he bumped against one of the

boxes himself, almost knocking it over. He reached out and held it in place, worried that the noise might be heard from the house, and then he took a few seconds to budge the box over onto a small table so that it would be more secure.

Nearby, another faint knock indicated that the cat was close.

"I'm something of a local historian," Henry said, deliberately keeping his back turned to the animal before slowly turning to take a look. "Like my father, and his father before him. In fact, my family has a very strong connection with the area."

He waited.

"You remember my grandfather, don't you?" he added, his voice tense with anticipation as he tried to work out exactly where the cat was hiding. "Oh, I think you do. I think you probably remember a great deal. His name was David. David Overton. He was a very good man, although to be honest I didn't get as much time with him as I would have liked. You see, I was still quite young when he died. When he was *taken* from me."

He took a step forward, causing a floorboard to creak gently beneath his weight.

"But again," he continued, "you know all about that." He paused once more, listening out for any hint of the cat's location. "I'm sure you know all too well. But I know a lot of things too, because at the end of his life my old grandfather told me all about his visits to this house. I know exactly what went on here back in the day."

As he continued to wait, he had no idea that the black cat – having set the dead mouse down – had stepped out from behind one of the boxes and was staring intently at the back of his head.

CHAPTER THIRTEEN

"THEY'RE REALLY BEAUTIFUL, AREN'T they?" Alison said as she finished hanging the crystals in her bedroom. She took a step back while admiring the way light caught on the edges. "I honestly don't know if I could live without them."

"That's great, Mum," Parker replied, barely even trying to hide her lack of interest as she stood in the doorway. "So now we've established that I didn't hide your crystals, and that I'm not generally engaged in some nefarious plot to ruin your life and mental well-being, can I please get back to the oh-so-fascinating task of scraping dried paint from the outside of the house?"

"You're being sarcastic," Alison said, turning to her.

"You think?"

"You shouldn't put that kind of negative energy out into the universe," Alison continued, stepping over to her and putting a hand on each of Parker's cheeks, then pulling gently in an effort to make her smile. "It just bounces right back at you and turns you into a grumble-guts."

"Mum -"

"And it makes you... harder to empathize with."

"Thank you. That makes me feel so much better." She pulled away so that her mother could no longer try to distort her face. "I'm not trying to put negative energy out into the universe, I'm just trying to get on with things. And it really doesn't help when you seem convinced that I'm hiding your crystals or... whatever else it is that you think I'm up to."

"You should try to relax."

"No-one ever relaxed because they'd been told to," Parker pointed out. "Think about it for a moment."

"Why don't we go out for something to eat?" Alison asked, stepping closer and grabbing her daughter's hands. "You and me, like the old days. I bet there are tons of quaint little country pubs in the area, and we should probably get to know the locals. After all, I'm determined to connect with other businesses in the area, and I'm sure some networking wouldn't go amiss."

"Mum, you just said -"

"That settles it!" Alison added excitedly, stepping past her and hurrying to one of the other rooms. "Let me just grab a few things, and then we're off for a meal!"

"Okay, sure," Parker replied, fully aware that she should sound more grateful. She knew her mother was planning to bore her to death over a couple of burgers, but at the last moment she realized that there were probably worse ways to spend an afternoon. Such as scraping old paint off the side of the house. "I'll get my shoes."

***

"Pussycat?" Henry whispered, stepping through the darkness of the garage, his right foot knocking some old discarded broken glass in the process. "Pussycat, where are you? I know you're in here, I saw you squeezing through that hole."

He paused again, waiting for some hint of the cat's location.

"I know what you are," he added finally, dropping any pretense of friendliness. "You don't seriously think that anyone round here's going to stand for more nonsense, do you? You're just a leftover. You realize that, don't you? You're a stray strand left behind at the end of a story that ended a long time ago. The fact that you're still here at all is extremely pathetic, but then... I've never been a cat person."

He looked over his shoulder, watching the shadows.

"I prefer dogs," he sneered, "and -"

Before he could finish, he heard voices outside. Worried that he was about to be discovered, he hurried to the far wall and peered through a crack; he saw the two women leaving the house, with the older woman rambling on about something while the younger girl – the daughter, he assumed – trailed a little way behind. There was nothing particularly objectionable about these two women, save for the fact that they'd made the huge mistake of moving into Styre House, but Henry knew he couldn't really hold that against them. They were just a pair of bumbling idiots.

"This one in Almsford looks perfect," the older woman said as she climbed into the car. "I don't know about you, but I'm absolutely starving. I just hope there isn't lots of coriander on the menu, I hate that stuff with a passion."

"Give me strength," the younger woman muttered, stopping for a moment and looking toward the sky as if engaged in a moment of prayer. "Please don't let me strangle my own mother."

Henry waited as the woman sat in the car, and then as the vehicle's engine rumbled to life. He watched as the car reversed along the driveway, and as it drove out of sight he could barely believe his luck at all. Having hoped to merely snoop around a little, he'd arrived at Styre House at the absolute most perfect moment imaginable; the inhabitants had headed out, clearly discussing plans to eat somewhere, which meant that he had free rein to take a look around the property at his leisure.

He glanced around the garage one more time, but he still saw no sign of the cat. He spotted a strange dark patch near the far wall, but he gave no thought to that as he picked his way past the boxes and exited the garage, stepping back out into the afternoon sunlight.

At that moment his phone briefly buzzed, and he saw that he had a message from Colin asking when he'd be back.

"Later," he muttered out loud as he typed that word, before sending the message and then slipping his phone away.

Walking past the end of the garage, he finally dared to approach the house itself. He made his way straight over to the spot where the car had been parked, but his attention was entirely drawn to the house, which until that moment he'd never visited up close; he'd seen the place from the road, of course, and he'd looked at plenty of photos, but he'd never really dared to trespass on the property. Now, however, he felt utterly emboldened, and as he stopped and looked up at the windows he was struck by the atmosphere of the place, which seemed strangely calm.

In stark contrast, he noted, to its history.

Looking down at the ground, he realized that once – many years earlier – his grandfather had most likely stood on the exact same patch of gravel.

"Lydia Smith," he said with a faint smile as he turned to the house again. "We meet at last. Well, we don't meet, because you're long gone, but you get the gist."

He took a deep breath.

"I feel so stupid," he continued. "I've spent all these years living in fear, but there's nothing here, is there? Nothing bad, anyway."

He let out a loud, relieved sigh.

"There *was* something," he added. "Oh yes, I have no doubt of that. This house was once the home of a very dark and powerful presence, one that caused a lot of harm. But it's gone now, because some very brave men came here once and did what needed to be done. They cleansed the place. I'm surprised they didn't burn it down, frankly, but I suppose they had their reasons."

Pausing for a moment, he felt a sudden wave of sadness running through his chest.

"My poor grandfather," he whispered, "would have had a very different life if it hadn't been for this house. In the years after he came here, he seemed increasingly haunted by what had happened. Then again, you can't change the past, can you? You can only remember it and honor it, and try to avoid making the same mistakes again."

Hearing a rustling sound, he turned to see that the black cat had emerged from the garage and was slowly making its way closer.

"But *you're* still here," he continued. "How does it feel to be without your mistress? Hmm? It must be a kind of purgatory for you, trapped here and never able to leave, forced to just slink about." He crouched down and watched as the cat, which was purring now, approached at its own meandering pace. "I can't believe I actually believed all those stories," he chuckled. "To hear it told, you were some big fearsome old monster, almost as dangerous as your former mistress. But look at you. You're just a puny little cat, stuck endlessly hunting for mice in some sad purgatory."

The cat brushed against his leg, pushing for a moment before easing past.

"You might not even be the same cat," Henry added with a smile. "Now there's a thought, eh? You might just be another random black stray that ended up here. The original Smythe might be long gone and -"

Suddenly the cat jumped up onto his shoulders from behind. Startled, Henry almost got to his feet, but instead he waited as the cat rubbed one side of its face against his ear.

"Oh, don't try being cute with me, young man," he continued, although he had to concede that he was quite enjoying the attention. "Yes, there's nothing remotely scary about you, is there? I don't think you're Smythe after all, I think that was an absolute load of old poppycock." He chuckled again as the cat reached around to his throat with one paw. "I actually can't believe that I ever allowed myself to be scared by a stupid little cat!"

He started laughing, but at that moment the cat sliced its claw across Henry's throat, cutting the flesh open and bringing a torrent of blood immediately gushing from the wound.

CHAPTER FOURTEEN

"STYRE HOUSE?" THE BARMAN said, furrowing his brow as he walked over to the pumps and began to pour a pint of beer. "Yeah, I know the place. Everyone round here knows Styre House. You might even say that it's got something of a reputation."

"I hope it does," Alison replied, leaning against the bar and twiddling some strands of hair between her fingers. "We're going to be using that reputation to try to get some publicity drummed up once the place is ready for its grand reopening. You don't happen to have any contacts in the local newspaper business, do you?"

She waited for an answer, but after just a few seconds she began to realize that the barman had fallen strangely quiet, as if he really didn't want to talk too much at all. Indeed, the few other people drinking in the pub that lunchtime had also stopped talking, and Alison couldn't help but feel as if everyone was now listening to hear what she might say next. She glanced around nervously as a few people cleared their throats, and she felt sure that anything she said now would almost certainly be taken the wrong way.

"Well, we're still... formulating our plans," she stammered, hoping to avoid lengthening the awkward silence. She waited again, but she was starting to feel more and more irritated by the villagers' reactions. "Okay, fine," she muttered, tapping her card against the machine and then taking the drinks. "Sorry I said anything."

"Did you just have an argument with the barman?" Parker asked as her mother sat opposite her in the booth. "Or was that your weird way of flirting?"

"It wasn't an argument," Alison said firmly, "and I most certainly wasn't flirting. These country bumpkins obviously have some sort of hatred for outsiders. The welcome was like something straight out of a horror film, and I really can't be bothered dealing with their negative energy." She took a sip of beer. "If I hadn't already ordered our lunch, I'd be inclined to find somewhere else to eat."

"Not all the locals are like that," Parker told her.

Nearby, another post advertised the activities of the Almsford Historical Reenactment Society, which seemed to be very busy in the local area.

"Are you talking about your boyfriend?" Alison asked.

"He's not my boyfriend," she insisted, beyond annoyed by her mother's insinuation. "Believe me, there's definitely nothing romantic there." She took a sip from her own glass, trying to get a few seconds of precious thinking time. "Do you ever feel like we've come in at the end of a story?" she continued, lowering her voice a little so that they wouldn't be overheard. "I'm starting to think that the history of that house might be more relevant than either of us realized."

"Then it's just as well that the local yokels aren't my target customer base," Alison opined archly. "Most of these people can barely afford clean clothes. They certainly wouldn't be able to pay for a night at my holistic dream therapy retreat."

"Is that what you're planning now?"

"My precise goals are fluid," Alison told her, reaching up and adjusting the patch over her left eye. "That's the sign of a good businesswoman, you know. You have to be able to duck and dive, and react to the market."

"What's a holistic dream therapy retreat

when it's at home, anyway?"

"You'll find out in due course."

"Can't I find out now, Mum? After all, I'm the poor idiot who's going to get press-ganged into helping out when it inevitably goes tits up. Seriously, I'm not a complete moron. If you tell me about your plans, I might actually be able to suggest some good ideas."

"A genius doesn't need advice," Alison told her haughtily. "Trust me, Parker. I know when I'm cooking good stuff."

"Uh-huh," Parker replied, as she saw a hint of something dark soaking through from beneath the eye-patch. "Mum, are you *sure* you shouldn't get that checked out? Is it oozing?"

"It's fine!" Alison hissed, before glancing around as she realized that the locals had begun to pick up on her raised voice. "It's fine," she said again, more quietly this time. "It's just an allergy, that's all. Now can we please get these drinks drunk? Once the food has arrived, I want to wolf it down and then never set foot in this wretched small-minded little country pub again."

***

"No, I'm just taking Woodbine out for his lunchtime constitutional," Fenella Bottomley said, speaking into her phone as she wandered along the country lane. "You know what he's like if he doesn't get some exercise around the middle of the day, and at least this way he should sleep all afternoon before you take him to the pub."

Glancing over her shoulder, she saw her middle-aged hound sniffing the grass verge.

"Come along, Woodbine!" she called out before setting off again. "Sorry, I was just talking to the dog," she continued. "I don't know what he finds so interesting in all this grass, to me it all looks the same but he follows that nose of his as if it's the most fascinating thing in the world. Things really are different for dogs, aren't they? Sometimes I wonder how they perceive the world around us!"

Already getting left behind, Woodbine was busy sniffing the ground, following a trail as he approached the driveway leading to Styre House. He glanced along the driveway and began to hurry past, before stopping as he heard a faint gasping sound. With his tail still held high, he looked toward the house and waited, and after a moment he saw something very slowly crawling around from behind a nearby bush.

"Help!" Henry Overton gasped, reaching out toward the dog with one hand while clutching his torn throat with the other, trying to stop more blood gushing from his wound. "Please," he continued as thunder rumbled in the distance. "Get help!"

Shocked by the sight of the man, Woodbine

merely stood and stared at him, although slowly his tail was dropping down as he began to understand that something was seriously wrong.

"Please," Henry sobbed, struggling to haul himself forward now as he tried to get some air into his lungs. "For the love of... please, I... I need help, I need..."

"Woodbine?" Fenella shouted in the distance. "Woodbine, come along!"

The dog turned and saw that his owner was at the junction. He watched her waving for a moment, and then he let out a brief bark in an attempt to let her know that her attention was required.

"Oh, don't be silly!" Fenella continued. "Woodbine, there's going to be rain soon. Do you want to be out in that? Of course you don't! You'll get all muddy and then you'll need a shower when we go home. You hate showers. Come along, you silly little mutt!"

With that she took the left turn, stepping out of view.

Woodbine turned to look at Henry again, and he saw that the injured man had managed to drag himself a little further along the driveway. A fraction of a second later, however, a black cat stepped into view, reaching out with ruthless efficiency and digging the claws of one paw into Henry's cheek; letting out a pained groan, Henry tried to pull away, but this only caused the claws to start slicing through his face.

After a few seconds, the cat slowly turned and stared at Woodbine with a pair of fierce yellow eyes.

Woodbine, in response, started growling at the cat.

"Help me," Henry whimpered, as fresh blood ran from the cuts on his cheek and started dribbling down the steps. "Get help! Can you do that? Please, it's life or death. Fetch help! Go! Good dog! Get help!"

Still growling, Woodbine took a step forward, only for the cat to let out an angry hiss. Terrified, the dog pulled back all the way out onto the road. The cat, meanwhile, was still hissing, and finally Woodbine was the one to back down. Turning around briefly, the dog let out a brief whimper before turning and hurrying away along the road, desperately trying to catch up to his owner.

"No, don't go!" Henry cried, as heaving sobs threatened to grip his body entirely. "No, please, you can't go! Wait... you *must* go! Good boy! You have to get help! Fetch help! Please!"

Turning, he looked up at the cat and felt a shiver run through his chest. Still clutching his throat, he tried to stop more blood seeping out between his fingers.

"Why are you doing this?" he gasped. "*How*

are you doing this? You're just... you're only a..."

His voice trailed off, and after a few more seconds he let out one final sigh before falling unconscious, letting his head bang against the driveway's gravel in the process.

The cat stared at Henry for a moment, before purring as he turned and walked down toward his feet. Henry remained unconscious on the driveway as a few light spots of rain began to fall, but a moment later his body began to slide back behind the hedge, as if some hidden force was slowly dragging him toward the garage.

CHAPTER FIFTEEN

"THIS RAIN IS HORRIBLE!" Alison shouted around an hour later, as she stepped out of the car and held her coat over her head so she could try to reach the front door without drowning. "I didn't know it was going to be this bad!"

"Welcome to the countryside," Parker muttered, climbing out of the car and slamming the door shut, then taking shelter under a tree for a moment. "At least there'll be no more scraping, not in this weather."

Down at her feet, the rain was washing the last of Henry's unnoticed blood away into a nearby flower border.

"Welcome to misery," Parker continued, watching as her mother continued to struggle with the key. "This is my life from now on, isn't it? Rain and mud and countryside weirdness and..."

Her voice trailed off as she saw the broken gravestone still poking up from the ground. Tilting her head, she couldn't help but feel that the gravestone was far more noticeable now, almost as if it was poking out a little further from the mud. She knew that was unlikely, of course, and that there was no kind of sub-soil pressure that could be forcing the stone up, but at the same time she couldn't shake the feeling that the stone was now a little more visible.

Hearing a bumping sound, she turned and looked toward the garage. With rain pounding down and battering every possible surface, the air was already filled with a kind of constant hissing sound, but for a moment Parker felt as if she could hear something else, as if she could just about make out a bumping noise coming from the garage. She knew that shouldn't be the case, in fact she was fairly sure that neither she or her mother had entered the garage since their arrival, but as she looked at the dirty windows of the squat little building she couldn't help but wonder what might really be going on inside, and she made a mental note to find a way through the door once the weather was better.

"Parker!" Alison called out from the house's front door. "Are you coming in or not? I need help moving that sofa!"

"On my way!" Parker shouted, before

hurrying toward the house, taking a short-cut across the grass. "You don't have to be so -"

Suddenly her left foot caught on something and she fell, landing hard on the ground with a pained gasp. Having almost twisted her ankle, she reached down and touched the side of her foot, checking for damage; she was already soaked now and the palms of her hands were covered in dirty gravel, but a moment later she looked at the gravestone fragment that had tripped her and she realized that it seemed to have changed yet again; somehow the damn thing appeared to have jutted up even further from the ground, as if in the space of a few short minutes some unseen force had thrust it a little further out of the ground.

"Parker, what are you doing?" Alison asked, appearing in the doorway again. "Why are you out there on the ground in the pouring rain? Have you completely lost your mind?"

"To be honest," Parker muttered, picking herself up and heading to the door, "I think I might have done."

"What were you doing down there on the ground?"

"Nothing," she continued, very much keen to avoid setting her mother off with any talk of weirdness. "I just tripped, that's all. So where's this sofa and why does it need moving?"

***

Letting out a faint, pained gasp, Henry Overton somehow found the energy to roll onto his back. He'd already lost a lot of blood, and his right hand – held against his torn throat for so long – was now almost kept in place by sticky blood that had begun to dry around the wound. Trying desperately to get some air into his lungs, he lay staring up at the garage's roof as he contemplated his next move.

A moment later he heard a bumping sound coming from somewhere in the darkness nearby.

"Wait," he groaned, barely able to get any words out at all. "Stop. Please, you have to stop. I'm begging you... leave me alone..."

The sound continued, moving around him a little and seemingly edging closer to his head.

"What do you want?" he continued. "How -"

Before he could finish, he felt a thud on his chest, and he looked down just in time to see that the black cat was now sitting on him. Unable to push the creature away, Henry could only watch in horror as he stared up into its eyes.

"You!" he hissed. "I've seen you before! You *are* the one from the photos, aren't you? I've heard rumors about you. Some people think it's impossible, I used to be one of them, but I know better now. You're him. You're the same cat that's in all the pictures. You're Smythe."

The cat tilted his head slightly, as if he recognized his name.

"So what are you doing here?" Henry asked, playing for time as he tried to work out what he could use as a weapon. "Your mistress is long gone. She died more than a century ago, so why don't you just get the message and follow her to Hell? Why are you still lingering here after so long? Go and find Lydia Smith so that you can burn together!"

The cat tilted his head the other way.

"Whatever you want," Henry continued, "you won't get it. If you're really him, then you must remember what happened last time. The people of this parish rose up against your mistress and ended her wicked ways. All of that happened long before I was born, but I've heard the tales. Everyone in the parish knows the story of Lydia Smith and -"

Suddenly the cat let out a loud, angry hiss.

"You don't like that, do you?" Henry said, reaching out with his left hand and feeling a small spade, which he realized could easily be turned into a weapon. He began to pull the spade closer while trying to avoid arousing suspicion. Fully aware that he'd only get one chance to strike, he realized that he needed to keep the cat's focus. "I know Lydia Smith was your mistress. Have you stuck around out of some misguided loyalty to her? You know she's dead and buried, right? My grandfather and men like him put her in the ground where she belongs. You might remember him. David Overton was -"

The cat hissed again, as if genuinely angered by the sound of that name.

"Lydia Smith was a witch," Henry sneered. "She was an abomination, and an affront to every decent person who ever lived. What she represented was nothing less than pure, unadulterated evil." He began to hold the spade up, ready to slice it straight through the cat's neck; his plan was nothing less than full decapitation to make sure that the wretched thing finally died. "Everyone knew that," he continued as he prepared to strike. "I'm sure she protested her innocence. I'm sure the lies flowed easily from her mouth, but she wasn't fooling anyone. She was a scourge on this village, a plague in human form, and everyone here was better off with her dead."

He adjusted his grip on the shovel, and he knew now that he had to strike soon.

"And you," Henry whispered, "are overdue to go and be reunited with -"

Suddenly the cat turned and lashed out with one paw, slicing across Henry's wrist. Letting out a gasp of pain, Henry tried to stab the cat with the spade, but instead the garden tool fell hopelessly from his hand; he tried to pick it up, but the cat had expertly cut the tendons in his wrist, rendering him unable to control his hand at all.

"Damn you!" he hissed. "What kind of infernal -"

Before he could finish, he felt something crawling up his body. Panicking, he tried to pull away, only to feel more and more of the strange creatures moving up over his waist and onto his chest. After a moment, making their way either side of the black cat, scores of dead mice reached Henry's neck and began to clamber onto his face, quickly forcing their way into his mouth. The more he tried to cry out, the more Henry's mouth opened wide to let the mice inside, and hundreds were now swarming onto his face. He struggled frantically, but the mice – all of them carrying the deadly wounds inflicted upon them – simply ignored his efforts and pushed deeper into his mouth, disappearing down the back of his throat as they began to fill his body.

Tilting his head back as more mice surged into his mouth, and feeling their dead claws scratching against his lips, Henry could no longer breathe as he felt the furry bodies wriggling their way into his stomach. As tears filled his eyes, he began to shudder violently, but the black cat remained calmly on his chest, watching with a sense of curious ease as the dying man twitched and breathed his final breath.

CHAPTER SIXTEEN

"HAS ANYONE SEEN HENRY?" Colin asked as he made his way through the crowded pub, trying to reach the bar. "Sorry, I don't mean to bother you, but has anyone seen Henry Overton this evening? I've been trying to contact him but -"

"Mind out," a man grumbled, almost spilling his pint as Colin tried to squeeze past. "Watch where you're going."

"Sorry," Colin mumbled, twisting first one way and then the other as he finally managed to get to the bar, where he found the landlord waiting for him. "Sorry," he continued, "I didn't mean to cause a -"

"Drink?" the landlord asked gruffly.

"No, thank you, I only -"

"You'll have to have a drink if you want to

be here," the man said, grabbing a glass and starting to pour Colin a pint of ale "It's not free for me to have the radiators on, you know."

"I'm sure," Colin said, "but I really don't like beer very much. Or most alcohol."

"I'm pouring it now," the landlord pointed out. "What do you expect me to do? Chuck it away?"

"No, but -"

"Get that down your neck," the man continued, sliding the pint over to him. "You'll enjoy it, you know. It's a good brew from barely twenty miles down the road. Should put some hair on your chest."

"Right," Colin replied, "but -"

"That'll be five of your pounds and eighty of your pennies, please."

"Well, I..."

Colin's voice trailed off for a moment, but he already knew that he couldn't exactly refuse. Reaching into his pocket, he took out his wallet and found his bank card, and then he tapped the reader that the landlord had helpfully held out for him.

"Thank you," Colin continued, "but -"

"You were asking about Henry Overton?"

"He was supposed to come back to the hub before closing time, but he didn't show up," Colin explained, clutching his newfound copy of *Local Paranormal Mysteries* by an author named James

Ward. "I'm sure nothing's wrong, but I've been doing some more research into Styre House and I really think Henry would be interested in what I've found. I've tried his mobile, but it's switched off or out of range of a tower, and I've tried knocking on his door but there's no sign of him. I know he likes coming in here, so I just thought that maybe someone might have seen him."

He waited for a reply, but he could already tell that he wasn't making much of a good impression.

"Drink," the landlord said firmly.

"Oh, I -"

"Drink."

"Right." Looking down at the pint, Colin realized that he had no choice. He lifted the glass to his lips, and then he took a sip, immediately disliking the taste. He knew he couldn't let this dislike show, however, so he forced himself to swallow several times before setting the glass back down. To his surprise, he saw that he'd managed to drink almost a third. "Wow."

"Good stuff, eh?" the landlord suggested.

"It certainly has a distinctive taste," Colin admitted, before furrowing his brow. "And an even more unusual aftertaste. Listen, I'm really sorry to bother you, I don't need to keep you for long. Are you saying that you haven't seen Henry at all this evening?"

"He hasn't been in," the landlord said firmly. "Which is odd, actually, because he doesn't miss many days." He checked his watch. "He'd have been in by now if he was coming, though. *University Challenge*'s on soon and he wouldn't want to miss that, and he wouldn't want to rush his pint, either. So I can confidently suggest that we won't be seeing him tonight, in which case he's almost certainly at home. Aren't you going to finish your pint?"

"I already tried knocking on his door," Colin explained, before – under pressure – taking another long sip of ale. "I'm sure it's fine. He's probably just busy, that's all. I suppose what I've got to tell him can wait until tomorrow."

***

Making his way along the dark, sloping street that led back to his mother's house, Colin stopped for a moment at the bus shelter to get a break from the rain.

He looked over at the cottages opposite, and he saw that Henry's place was still unlit. He had no idea where Henry might have gone, but he supposed that he shouldn't simply assume that the older man had no life; for all he knew, Henry was off on a hot date somewhere, or meeting some friends, and he figured that he'd show up the next day with some fascinating stories. As rain continued to batter the bus shelter's roof, Colin let out a heavy sigh as he realized that he was simply going to have to make a run for his mother's front door, and that more likely than not he was going to get soaked in the process.

"Three," he whispered, "two -"

Suddenly spotting movement in the darkness, he peered at Henry's cottage. The place was still dark, but as he continued to watch he realized that he could just about make out a figure standing at the window. His first thought was that he must be mistaken, that there was no reason why Henry would be lurking in his own front room with no lights on, but as the seconds passed the image became a little clearer. From the silhouette alone, Colin was fairly sure that this must be Henry, and he couldn't shake the sense that something seemed to be very wrong. Finally, realizing that there was no sign of a let-up in the weather, he hurried across the street and into Henry's garden, and then he took shelter under the slight overhang above the window.

"Henry, is that you?" he called out, trying to make sure that he could be heard above the rain. "Henry, are you okay in there?"

He waited, but Henry was merely staring out now from inside the dark cottage.

"Henry, it's me," Colin continued, waving gingerly before gently tapping the window. "It's Colin."

Again he waited.

Again, Henry simply stared out from inside the room.

"It's Colin from the history hub," he added, even though he and Henry knew one another extremely well already. "I just... I've been trying to find you all evening, I did some more research on Styre House and I found a rather interesting old book, and I just want to run a few ideas past you so that..."

His voice trailed off, and after a moment Henry simply took a step back, disappearing into the darkness.

"Okay," Colin continued, furrowing his brow, puzzled by the older man's behavior. "That's fine. If you don't want to talk, I get it. I can just... catch you tomorrow at the hub."

After a few seconds he leaned closer to the window, cupping his hands around his eyes in an attempt to see inside. Unable to make anything out at all, he pulled back; part of him wanted to bang on the door until Henry opened up, but in truth he'd always felt that Henry had something of a darker side, and he told himself that perhaps his colleague was simply engaged in some kind of weird hobby. Either that, or – as Colin had long suspected – Henry was part of some weird erotic role-playing society. Whatever the truth, he knew from experience that he was fiercely private and that he wouldn't take kindly to any kind of intrusion.

"As long as you're okay, then," he continued cautiously, figuring that he'd given Henry more than enough time to ask for any necessary help. "I was going to tell you something about Styre House, but it's nothing that can't wait until the morning. To be honest, you probably know half of it, anyway. You've always been so much more knowledgeable about local history than me, given... well, given that your family's got roots round here for..."

Realizing that he was rambling, he resolved to simply leave Henry alone. After a moment he stepped over to the front door and posted the book through the letterbox.

"Right," he added. "Message understood, loud and clear. I'll see you tomorrow."

Swallowing hard, he stared at the dark window and realized that – for whatever reason – Henry most certainly wasn't in the mood to answer. After contemplating a few other things that he might try to say, he turned and headed out of the garden; he glanced back one last time, wondering whether Henry was quite alright, and then he hurried on his way, determined to get home and do some more research before dinner. He still couldn't quite ignore a faint sense of concern, but he told himself that Henry was clearly alright, even if he appeared to be in a bit of a funny mood. Which wouldn't be the first time.

Back at the cottage, rain continued to lash the window as Henry leaned closer to the glass. He reached out and touched the pane, clearly puzzled, and then he used the same hand to touch his own face.

"No, please," he sobbed, "I can't be dead. Anything but this. Please, somebody help me. I don't want to be dead. I'm too young. Please, somebody get me out of here!"

CHAPTER SEVENTEEN

RAIN WAS STILL FALLING at Styre House as Parker lay on her bed with the lights off, staring – as usual – at her phone. With her face bathed in the screen's glow, she continued to scroll through random celebrity news sites while telling herself that soon she was actually going to switch off and get some sleep.

Nearby, the black cat was purring as he slept happily.

"You're better off out of this stuff," Parker muttered as rain continually peppered the window. "Sometimes I wish I could come back as a cat, and that way I wouldn't have to know anything about celebs or all their nonsense."

She clicked through to another page and took a moment to scan the headlines.

"I know I'm addicted," she continued. "Some people are just born with magnetism, aren't they? And others, like yours truly, are born with the opposite of that. Like, I'm under no illusion that I'm interesting or pretty or special in any conceivable way. I don't have any talents. What do I have to offer? Sometimes I think I'm just a waste of space, doomed to float through life without contributing to anything. I'm not even smart. I mean, usually someone like me would at least have two brain-cells to rub together, but I'm a loser in that department as well."

She scrolled down and saw a before-and-after shot of a reality star, highlighting the extreme amount of cosmetic work that she'd had done.

"Maybe I need a new look," she sighed. "Maybe I should go all-in and try to become some kind of glamour girl. I'd need a *lot* of work, but this body of mine isn't anything to write home about."

She heard thunder rumbling in the distance, but she kept her eyes on the screen even as the black cat turned and looked toward the window.

"I'd gladly swap it," Parker murmured. "That's so pathetic, isn't it? It's also true. Then again, I'm a blotchy-skinned mildly overweight girl. Even that Colin guy probably has better offers. Who in their right mind would ever want -"

Suddenly a louder crack of thunder rang out, shaking the window, and the cat immediately sprang up and jumped off the bed. Parker turned and watched as he raced out of the room and hurried downstairs, and then she turned to look at her phone again.

"Good idea," she muttered. "I'm going to go to sleep soon, anyway. I'll just check out a few more headlines first." She found another page showing lots of shots of celebrities with various procedures that had mucked up their faces. "I'm really nothing special," she continued, as she tapped to play a video, with the sound pumping into her headphones. "Who'd ever want *me*?"

***

"Damn it," Alison sighed, sitting on the sofa and scratching once more at her arm. "What the hell is going on in this house? What's making me so damn itchy?"

With her laptop propped open, showing the latest episode of a crime show in one window and some spot-popping videos in another, she kept her eyes on the screen while absent-mindedly scratching her arm some more. She heard another rumble of thunder outside – the third, she was dimly aware – but she didn't even bother to look at the window. Far more interested in the videos playing on the screen, she failed to even notice that her constant scratching was starting to draw blood around her elbow.

She also failed to notice movement over by the doorway. The black cat hurried into view and then stopped to stare at her for a moment; barely visible in the low light, the cat kept his eyes fixed on Alison as she continued to scratch her arm, and then after a moment the animal turned and walked away, swiftly disappearing into the kitchen.

"Parker?" Alison said, suddenly looking across the room, as if at the last second she'd picked up on something. "Is that you?"

She waited, but there was no sign of anyone and the only sound came from rain still tapping at the window.

"Parker, are you downstairs?" Alison continued. "Honey, could you fetch me another glass of wine from the kitchen? Parker? Please, you know I'm not lazy, I'd do it myself but I'm just so comfortable. Parker, are you there? I know I'm being a terrible pain in the backside, but my legs are aching and I don't want to get up."

She waited.

"Parker?"

Sighing, she set the laptop aside and got to her feet, before hauling herself through to the darkened kitchen. She kept the lights off as she wandered over to the counter, where she took a moment to pour some more wine into her glass from the box on the side. As she did so, she heard thunder rumbling again; she looked over at the window and listened to the rain, and she told herself that the plants in the garden would certainly be glad of the wet weather.

Once her glass was full, she turned and headed back to the front room. She yawned as she got back into position on the sofa; within seconds she was once more fully absorbed in the two videos, with the sound turned up to the maximum, to the extent that she failed to even notice the sound of the cat meowing loudly just beyond the window.

***

Rain was crashing down outside in the darkness, battering the trees and turning the ground into a thick muddy bog. The downpour was relentless once again, already forming small puddles in the mud, and those puddles had been slowly growing for a while now, threatening to become rivers of dirty water.

Meowing again, the black cat paced back and forth in the rain, seemingly paying no heed to the fact that he was getting wetter and wetter. Clearly agitated, the creature kept his gaze fixed on the broken piece of an old gravestone that was still poking up from the ground. After a few more seconds the piece of stone moved, wobbling slightly before shifting forward as if pushed from below.

Meanwhile the muddy ground all around was churning as if something was slowly starting to force its way up. Finally, after another clap of thunder, a piece of rotten wood began to emerge, followed by another and then another, followed a few seconds later by the unmistakable sight of a human hand reaching up from beneath the surface.

Watching from a few feet away, the black cat began to bawl loudly.

For the next couple of minutes, a shape slowly began to emerge from beneath the mud, forcing its way up while casting aside more and more chunks of rotten wood. The remains of the gravestone had been pushed fully to the side now, and the figure's arched back rose up toward the sky, quickly washed clean by the rain to reveal tattered fabric and rotten, partially-bare ribs. Thick, dirty water was already dribbling out between the bones, and a few seconds later a shape at the front of the figure began to lift up, revealing a skeletal face with matted black hair hanging down heavily on either side. The figure's jaw began to open, emitting a gurgled cry as more mud ran from the empty eye-sockets.

The cat moved closer, meowing louder still as he brushed against the figure's side.

Dragging itself fully out of the grave, the figure slowly but surely rose to its feet, swaying slightly as rain washed more mud away. Clearly unsteady, the figure stood in the rain as if it was waiting for all the mud to dribble down, leaving exposed sections of bone with patches of skin still clinging to some of the joints. The figure's faded dress, meanwhile, was riddled with gaping holes that revealed what remained of her skeletal body, and a few clumps of dirt were still tumbling out from the hollow cavern of her rib-cage. A few seconds later she held out her hands, as if taking a moment to feel the rain and mud dribbling through the gaps in her bones as she tilted her head to look up toward the sky.

Opening her mouth, she let out another mournful wail.

Down on the ground, the cat stepped closer and brushed once more against the side of her leg, before slinking away and heading toward the garage. Reaching the door, the cat turned and looked back through the rain, pausing for a moment before letting out a louder cry.

Turning slowly, the figure began to follow the sound of the cat's call, stumbling across the muddy ground and reaching out to support itself. As it reached the garage, the figure held out its right hand, but the heavy rain proved too much and after a moment the entire forearm fell away from what was left of the rotten elbow. The figure lowered the stump of its arm and stood for a moment in the rain, before turning toward the house and letting out one final, agonized gasp.

CHAPTER EIGHTEEN

A FEW DROPS FELL from the windowsill, glinting in the morning light. The rainstorm had finally ended a little before sunrise and now the history hub's doors were wide open as Colin sat going over another set of photocopies.

"Henry?"

"He's not here," Colin murmured, before looking up as Donald Fraser made his way inside. "Actually, I was going to call you later. Have you heard from him at all?"

"Not a peep," Donald admitted, stopping on the other side of the desk and shoving his hands into his pockets. "That rain was pretty monstrous last night, wasn't it? Still, the garden needed it. My mother always used to tell me that what's good for the grass is good for the soul."

He leaned forward a little and peered at the papers.

"Styre House?" he muttered. "What are you reading up on that old place for?"

"I met the people who've moved in."

"Do you think that's a good idea?" Donald asked. "Sorry, I'm sure they're lovely, but they really shouldn't be living there. Nobody should."

"It's not their fault that the council insisted on selling the place," Colin pointed out. "I guess they saw the chance to get a cheap deal and they went for it."

"Fair enough," Donald muttered with a shrug. "My parents always told me to stay away from the whole area around Styre House. They kept issuing ominous, vaguely non-specific warnings that never really made a great deal of sense. Still, they did the trick, because my friends and I were little brats but we never dared to go near that house. I suppose it was all just a load of guff and nonsense."

"Do you know the story of Lydia Smith?" Colin asked.

"The witch? Only the basics."

"I've dug up some more about her," Colin continued. "Obviously we have to be careful, because there are lots of layers of superstition built up around the whole thing, but one element keeps jumping out at me."

"Oh yes?" Donald replied. "And what might that be?"

"People kept insisting that Lydia Smith was trying to possess someone. Apparently, for reasons that are lost in the mists of time, she needed a new body. Supposedly she was using witchcraft in an attempt to find herself a new body and inhabit it. In fact, there are even claims that she might have succeeded at least once, and that the Lydia Smith who lived at Styre House was already a soul existing in a stolen body."

"Stolen bodies, eh?" Donald muttered. "That all sounds a little rich for my liking. Then again, nothing would really surprise me round these parts, not anymore." He turned to head out, before stopping and looking back over at Colin. "I'll tell you what *does* stand out at me from all that stuff I heard about Lydia Smith. She was always said to have a black cat at her side. What was its name again? Samuel? Smithers?"

"Smythe," Colin reminded him. "Yes, I've come across that. In fact, plenty of people have spotted the same cat over the years. At least, it seems to be the same cat."

"Rum old coincidence, eh?" Donald continued, clearly lost in thought for a moment. "I'll track Henry down some other time. I'm sure he's very busy. I've always had this sneaking suspicion that he's into some rather dodgy stuff with the fairer sex, if you know what I mean." He wandered out into the morning light. "Then again, good for him. If old Henry wants to teach the ladies a few new tricks, then why shouldn't he have some fun?"

"I'd rather not think about that," Colin said, as he began to sift through the papers once again. After a moment he stopped as he saw a photo of Styre House, complete with a grainy image of a black cat sitting near one of the bushes and seemingly glaring back at the camera. "If you're real," he continued, whispering under his breath as he tried to make sense of everything he'd uncovered so far, "then what's your deal? Why have you been hanging around at that house for all these years?"

***

"Mum, do you seriously not have keys for this garage door? Who even buys a property and then doesn't get all the keys? We have to get in here! We don't know what there might be!"

"I'm sure there's nothing," Alison called back to her. "Darling, can you please focus on what's important? The garden's so muddy this morning, I need you to help me move all this wood and stone that's turned up out of nowhere."

"There was a padlock before," Parker continued, "but now the door just seems stuck fast."

"Parker! A little help?"

"Fine," Parker replied, as her feet could be heard stomping away from the garage, "but one way or another, I'm getting through that door eventually. What if there's treasure in there? What if there's stuff we could use or sell? Mum, don't take this the wrong way, but your lack of basic curiosity is really starting to make me wonder."

Parker was still complaining as she walked away, but – as her voice faded into the distance – the garage's dark and dusty interior fell quiet. After a few seconds the black cat emerged from behind some boxes, having watched Parker through a gap in the wall, and now the animal made its way across the cracked floor before stopping to watch what was happening at the far end. Flicking his tail briefly, the cat seemed utterly engrossed as he observed his mistress kneeling on the floor over Henry Overton's ruptured body.

Having been overwhelmed by the army of dead mice, Henry had died with approximately two hundred of the rodents stuffed inside his corpse. The mice had stopped moving now, returning to their dead states, but the rotten woman was leaning over Henry's body and using the fingernails of her remaining hand to carve a set of symbols into the dead man's face. Taking her time, the rotten figure knew that she had to get the symbols just right if they were to work at all, and finally – once she was satisfied – she moved her hand onto Henry's chest and began to push down, forcing air from his lungs.

Still watching this arcane ritual, the cat slipped behind some tools so that he could remain unobserved as he edged closer.

Leaning down further, the rotten women moved her skeletal face closer to Henry's features. Unable to see anything since her eyeballs were gone, the woman had resorted to her other senses, even if these too were hardly in their optimal state; she opened her mouth and managed a faint groan as she moved her hand onto the side of Henry's face, and a thin dribble of saliva began to drop from her mouth, eventually landing on the corpse's cheek. So far, she felt that she'd got the symbols right, although she worried that she might be mis-remembering a few of the details from Old Mother Marston's books.

Smythe, meanwhile, had made his way closer still.

Gasping again, the rotten woman placed her hand over Henry's heart and waited. More saliva ran from her mouth, and she remained entirely focused on the corpse for a few seconds until – finally – Henry's body let out a brief, involuntary and somewhat mechanical jerk.

The cat pulled back a little, clearly nervous.

The rotten women pushed on Henry's chest again, bringing forth another jerk. She began to pound her rotten fist against his chest, as if she was trying to restart his heart, and any observer would likely have begun to notice a hint of desperation in the way she moved. She was almost shaking him now, as if she was trying to wake him up, but after a few more seconds she stopped and pulled back, emitting a guttural groan that seemed more like a sigh.

Having observed from a short distance, Smythe began to make his way forward, purring gently and -

Suddenly the rotten woman turned and snarled, and Smythe instantly raced away, disappearing behind some boxes. After a few seconds he poked his head back around from behind the boxes, watching as the rotten woman returned her attention to Henry's stricken corpse.

Shaking Henry once again, the woman seemed determined to somehow rouse him, even though his glassy dead eyes were staring up toward the ceiling. She shook him a little harder, then harder still, yet her efforts were clearly in vain as she began to bang a fist against the dead man's face. Finally she began to lift his head up, before cracking the back against the concrete floor several times as if she was trying to break the skull open and get to the brain and other prizes inside.

Smythe began to make his way closer again, trying to stay out of sight as he approached the woman's side. Purring again, he brushed against the woman as he slipped past, clearly trying to ingratiate himself.

In that moment, the woman angrily grabbed Smythe and threw him across the room, sending him screaming and crashing into the far wall. Letting out another harsh growl, the woman slammed her remaining fist against the ground in a furious but ultimately futile gesture of defiance and frustration.

Nearby, a terrified Smythe watched her fury with a growing sense of terror.

CHAPTER NINETEEN

"SO I REORGANIZED THE boxes down in the study," Parker said as she reached the door to her mother's bedroom, "and then I -"

Stopping suddenly, she saw that something was very wrong. Alison was flat on her back on the bed, breathing heavily and seemingly unaware that she had company. Filled with a distinct sense of dread, Parker made her way over and looked down, only to see that her mother seemed a little pale and sweaty.

"What's going on?" she asked. "Mum? I think it might be time for me to call a doctor."

"No!" Alison gasped, starting to sit up before losing the battle and slumping back down. "Sweetie, I'm fine, I just need to rest, that's all. I thought I was doing so well dealing with the stress, but now I realize that I was just storing up all the negative consequences for another day." Groaning, she struggled somewhat as she rolled onto her side, and finally she flopped down on her belly with her head at the foot of the bed. "This feels better," she continued, leaning over the side and staring down at the carpet. "I don't know why, but I feel much better in this position."

"Mum, I'm calling a -"

"No!" Alison hissed. "Don't you dare! I'm serious, this is my body and I make my own choices."

"Mum, I'm worried about you," Parker continued. "You've been wearing that patch over your eye for too long now and it's starting to look like something's bulging out from underneath. Meanwhile your skin's all red and itchy, it's like you're breaking out all over in sores. Enough's enough, okay? At some point you have to realize that something might actually be seriously wrong."

"I have allergies!" Alison countered.

"Not this badly, you don't," Parker said firmly. "No-one does. Mum, I'm just going to get someone to come out and take a look at you. If you're right and this is just caused by pollen or whatever, they probably have some antihistamines that'll help."

"So you want me to take unnatural chemicals manufactured by big pharmaceutical companies that only care about profit?"

"This isn't the time for a crusade," Parker said, rolling her eyes. "Antihistamines aren't exactly new or controversial. Just get some down your throat and you'll probably be fine."

"Not tonight," Alison murmured. "Parker, please, you know how I feel about mainstream medicine. Just let me rest here like this tonight, and I promise you that I'll be fine in the morning. But if for some reason I'm not, then I swear I'll let you call a doctor and I'll take whatever pills he prescribes. Do we have a deal or not?"

Parker opened her mouth to tell her mother that she was crazy, but at the last second she held back as she realized that she was never going to win this argument. Her mother was decidedly stubborn and would certainly refuse to cooperate with any doctor until the absolute last minute, so she told herself that her best bet was to accept the so-called deal and then call for help in the morning.

"Fine," she said with a sigh. "I'm not happy about it, but it's not like I can force you to do the right thing. If you're still like this tomorrow, though, you'd better believe that I'm putting my foot down and calling an ambulance. Whether you like it or not."

"Whatever, Parker," Alison stammered, as if she was struggling to remain conscious. "Just turn the light off and leave the door ajar when you go, okay? I need to rest and recuperate, and then I'm sure that I'll be so much better by tonight. Or, failing that, certainly by tomorrow morning. I know my own body."

"If you say so, Mum," Parker whispered under her breath. "But if you're still sick in the morning, you're going to get help whether you like it or not."

***

"This is insane," she said as she scrolled down the page, researching possible causes for her mother's various ailments. "There's no way it's allergies."

She clicked through to another page, but in truth she was getting tired and most of the information was simply washing over her without sticking. She knew she should go to sleep, but at the same time she felt extremely wired and she knew that the questions swirling through her head were going to keep her awake. Opening yet another page, she found herself on a forum for people with similar problems, although none of them exactly matched what was going on with her mother.

Hearing a creaking sound, she turned to see that her bedroom door was opening slightly, and sure enough a moment later the black cat jumped up onto the bed and began to make his way closer.

"You're back, huh?" Parker said, reaching

out and stroking Smythe's side. "Why do I get the feeling that you're starting to like hanging out?"

Purring, the cat pushed against her arm and then turned around as if to offer her another area for patting.

"I'm really worried about Mum," Parker continued. "I've been putting it out of my mind as much as possible, but I can't do that now. There's clearly something seriously wrong with her. The worst thing is that I'm pretty sure she agrees, but she's too scared to do anything about it."

Smythe rolled onto his back, playing cute as he exposed his belly.

"Not like you," Parker muttered. "You seem pretty healthy, don't you? Must be all those mice."

She turned back to look at her phone again, but the cat immediately let out a brief meow.

"You really want attention tonight, don't you?" Parker sighed. "Fine, whatever. Are you trying to make yourself part of the family?" She stroked his belly for a moment before moving her hand up and feeling the tattered collar around his neck. His purrs stopped, as if he was a little less sure now, and Parker could tell that he didn't really like anyone touching the collar. "It's okay," she whispered. "I'd never hurt you."

Realizing that Smythe would probably pull away if she tried to examine the collar, she settled for feeling the rough fabric, which seemed to be held together by thick twine. In fact, the collar felt less like a modern item from a pet store and more like something both very old and very homemade. She could tell that the collar wasn't particularly tight or secure, and that it might easily come off if pulled hard.

Suddenly Smythe rolled over onto his other side, slipping away slightly and then getting to his feet before turning and rubbing one side of his face against Parker's arm.

"I'd love to know what you're thinking," she told him. "Then again, I suppose the feeling's mutual."

She once again returned her attention to the phone, while absent-mindedly scrolling though endless posts on the online forum. Lost in thought, she was hoping to find some quick and easy solution to her mother's health problems, even though she already knew deep down that a doctor's visit was going to be necessary. As the cat continued to brush against her, Parker focused more and more on the phone while trying to come up with some sort of strategy for cajoling Alison to at least try an online consultation. And if -

"Ow!"

Suddenly feeling a sharp pain in her arm, Parker pulled away, shocked to see deep scratch marks just above her wrist. Smythe was already hurrying away as if he knew he'd done something wrong, quickly hopping off the bed and disappearing out to the landing.

"Dude, what the hell?" Parker gasped, shocked that the cat had – seemingly with no provocation at all – decided to give her a good clawing.

Peering more closely at her arm, she could already see a few beads of blood leaking from the four thick lines running through her flesh. The wound was even deeper than she'd realized, and she winced as she felt a slight stinging pain.

"What did I ever do to you, huh?" she muttered as she grabbed a tissue and wiped the blood away. "Stupid cat, coming in here and acting all cute, then turning into some kind of angry little wolverine. Like, seriously, did you never hear the advice to avoid scratching the hand that occasionally feeds you?"

Once she'd cleaned up the wound and tossed the tissues away, she looked back at her phone. She felt more than a little annoyed by the cat's behavior, but she was far more worried about her mother's health problems. In fact, she was so engrossed in her research that she failed to even notice as a fresh bead of blood leaked out from one of the scratches, running down to her elbow and then dripping onto the fabric of the bed.

CHAPTER TWENTY

CHEERING LOUDLY, THREE DRUNKARDS wandered along the dark country lane, staggering slightly as they tried to make their way home from the pub.

"Please," Henry Overton whispered, standing at the window and watching as the men walked past his cottage, "I'm right here. Please, can't somebody help me?"

He hurried to the door and tried to pull it open, only to find that he couldn't make the latch turn at all. He tried a couple more times, convinced that he was simply fumbling in the darkness, but finally he came to realize that something more serious was wrong; every time he'd tried to leave the cottage, he'd found his mind starting to fill with a kind of fog. He'd faced the same problem whenever he'd tried to turn on the lights, and now he felt as if some hidden force was trying to keep him trapped in darkness forever.

"Please," he continued as he heard the drunk cries receding into the distance. "I don't want to be here. I'm not... I'm not dead. I can't be dead."

He hesitated before stepping back from the door. Holding his hands up, he tried once again to convince himself that everything was fine, yet deep down he felt strangely disconnected from the world. Stepping over to the bottom of the stairs, he looked at the banister for a moment; he'd tried several times to touch the wooden post at the foot of the staircase, yet something had been holding him back. Now, focusing as hard as he could manage, he reached out and moved his hand toward the post.

To his horror, he saw that his fingers passed straight through the wood. Feeling no kind of sensation at all, he pulled back and tried to ignore the sense of panic raging in his chest. He tried to pick up the book that Colin had posted through the letterbox, but this too proved to be an impossible task.

"No," he stammered, "it's something else. There's some other explanation. I'm not dead. I can't be dead. If I was dead, then -"

Suddenly letting out a pained gasp, he clutched his chest and stepped back before vanishing from view, leaving the cottage's cramped front room once again dark and empty.

***

Opening its mouth and tilting its head back, Henry Overton's corpse let out a pained gasp. Its discolored hands reached up and touched its chest, and a series of labored groans began to escape from the back of its throat as the entire body shuddered slightly.

Leaning over the corpse, the rotten woman from the garden listened to the dead man's struggles.

"Help me," Henry said after a moment, turning to look around the darkened garage. "I'm not dead, I..."

His voice trailed off as he saw moonlight shining through a dirty window high up on the opposite wall.

"What happened?" he continued. "I was at home, I was back in my little cottage, and now suddenly I'm here and..."

His voice trailed off, and after a few seconds he looked up at the woman kneeling over him. He opened his mouth to ask her a million questions, but at that moment he saw her two empty eye-sockets staring back down at him, and he realized that he was staring into the face of what could only be death itself. He tried again to speak, but now he could feel something large obstructing his windpipe and he instinctively rolled over, coughing hard until he brought up the slimy, twisted remains of a dead mouse.

"No!" he gasped, pulling back a little as a few stray pieces of fur fell from his lips. Already, he could feel a strange heaviness in his belly. "What's happening to me? Please, I don't understand!"

Still listening to Henry's reaction, the dead woman let out a faint, disapproving groan.

Before he could get another word out, Henry started retching, quickly bringing up several more dead mice and spitting them onto the floor. He pulled back against the wall as his entire body shuddered, and after a moment he started reaching into his mouth, using his fingers to try to scrape out the small body parts that were constantly churning in the back of his throat. Tears were running down his face now and he couldn't help but let out a series of pained whimpering cries as he felt the pressure building behind his eyes.

"Somebody help me!" he managed to gasp finally. "I'm just an ordinary person, I never wanted any of this! What... I don't..."

Feeling a sharp pain in his chest, he looked down and saw that his shirt was hanging open. He pulled the two sides of fabric aside slowly and saw to his horror that some kind of pattern had been carved into his flesh, with thick cuts forming a series of non-concentric circles running all the way down as far as his belly. Although he'd never seen these patterns before, he could already tell that they carried some kind of logic, some form of internal discipline that suggested they were far from random.

"This shouldn't be happening to me," he sobbed. "It's not fair! I never hurt anyone, I never did anything to deserve this, why -"

Stopping suddenly, he realized that something else was wrong. He sat frozen in place for a moment, listening to the silence and feeling the stillness, and then he slowly put his hands on his chest. Too horrified to truly comprehend what he'd just noticed, he waited a few more seconds as a rising sense of panic and dread began to spread through his body.

"I'm not breathing," he whispered, before starting to frantically check the sides of his neck for a pulse. "Why am I not breathing? And why am I so cold? I feel like... I can feel that my blood's not flowing. I can feel my entire body isn't working. Why isn't my heart pumping? Why don't I need to breathe?"

Spotting movement, he turned to see that the rotten woman was limping closer.

"Stay back!" he screamed, turning and crawling behind some old doors that had been left leaning against a wall, desperate to find some kind of hiding place. "Leave me alone!"

Trying to make himself as small as possible, he began shaking violently as he felt again and again for a pulse. He told himself that he had to be wrong, that he couldn't be dead, but after a moment he started punching his own chest in one last desperate attempt to get his heart beating again.

"I just want to go home and be alive again," he sobbed, already feeling the tiny feet of more dead mice scratching at the back of his throat. "I should never have come out here in the first place, I should have kept my nose out of it all. I'm not a greedy man, I was happy with my life the way it was. God, if you just let me go back to being alive, I'll never do anything wrong again. I'll be good, I swear, and I'll always try to help others. I'll donate to charity and I'll volunteer more, I'll volunteer every second of every day. I'll donate all my spare money, and I'll stop drinking and I won't even eat carbs. I'll go to church if that's what it takes. I'll go to church every Sunday and I'll confess my sins, and I'll spend the rest of my life helping others. I'll stop going to the dungeon club in Aylesham! Please, I'll do all of that, but you have to let me live again!"

As Henry continued to splutter, calling out all sorts of promises, the rotten woman stood in the middle of the garage. She couldn't actually see Henry's feet poking out from behind the doors, but she could hear his desperate pleas and after a few seconds her shoulders dropped slightly as if she finally understood that her original plan wasn't working too well. A few seconds after that, hearing a scratching sound, she turned just as the black cat slipping back into the garage and made his way over.

Dropping down onto her knees, the woman reached out and stroked Smythe. Hearing his calm purr, she patted his side several more times, before he sat and looked over at the doors leaning against the far wall.

"I'll try other religions too, if that helps," Henry was sobbing. "It doesn't have to be one or the other. What if I try Christianity and Judaism and Islam and all the others, all at the same time? One of them has to be right, doesn't it? I'll just throw everything at the wall and see what sticks! Please, give me a sign!"

Smythe tilted his head, before turning to look up at the dead woman. He watched her face for a moment, seeing the sadness of her skeletal features, staring into the empty sockets that had once held her eyes. And then, slowly, he raised his right paw and extended his claws.

Letting out a faint groan, the woman turned away, but Smythe immediately let out another meow, as if deliberately trying to attract her attention. The woman turned to him again; stopping suddenly, she sniffed the air with what remained of her nose. After a few seconds she leaned forward, picking up the faint aroma of Parker's blood glistening on Smythe's claws.

She hesitated, and then she leaned closer still, as if attracted by some quality of the blood. And then, very slowly, she began to smile.

CHAPTER TWENTY-ONE

"I'M JUST RESTING!" ALISON called out from behind her bedroom door. "I feel a lot better this morning, Parker. I think I'm definitely turning a corner, and I just need to give myself a chance to relax. I'm going to spend the morning in bed and then I'll see how I feel at lunchtime."

"Okay," Parker said cautiously, trying the handle again, "but... why have you locked the door?"

"Have I? Oh, that must have been a mistake," Alison continued. "I got up to use the bathroom in the night, perhaps I instinctively locked it on my way back in. Silly me, I don't know why I did that."

"Can I come in?"

"That'd mean me getting up, Parker," Alison

complained, "which would defeat the whole purpose of resting. Listen, I wouldn't lie to you, I'm feeling so much better and I'm certain that by lunchtime I'll be back on my feet and ready to take on the world again. Just let me rest without nagging too much, okay?"

"If you're not up by lunchtime -"

"And don't give me arbitrary deadlines," Alison added, before coughing briefly. "Parker, I'll make a deal with you, okay? Just let me fully recuperate for the rest of the day and I promise you that if by tonight I'm still feeling even remotely poorly, I'll be on the phone to the doctor first thing tomorrow morning. Not that I'll need to, because you'll see that I'm quite alright. Do we have an arrangement, Parker?"

"I guess," Parker replied. "It's not like you're giving me much choice, is it? But you'd better stick to your side of this deal, Mum, or I'll..."

Pausing, she tried to think of some way she could back up that threat, although she realized after a few seconds that she was pretty helpless. She certainly wasn't about to start smashing down the bedroom door.

"I'll think of something," she added, turning and heading to the top of the stairs, only to stop as she spotted movement outside. Peering though the window, she couldn't deny a faint flicker of anticipation in her chest as she saw Colin leaning his bike against the wall. "Okay, stay cool," she continued, taking a deep breath. "He might be a little crazy, but I've got a feeling he's as good as it's gonna get round these parts. Time to make myself irresistible."

***

"That storm last night was crazy," Colin pointed out as he made his way along the garden path, looking around at all the mud. "It's done a real number here, hasn't it?"

"Totally," Parker replied, forcing a smile as she tried to think of something cool or interesting or funny to say.

"The gravestone's been completely ripped up," Colin continued, stopping and crouching down to examine the churned mud and the large chunk of stone. Spotting some pieces of rotten wood, he picked up a few chunks. "Did something happen here last night?"

"Like what?" Parker asked.

"I don't know, but it's like the ground's been all... disturbed."

"Storms can do that, right?" Parker suggested with a faint, nervous smile. "Do you want to come inside for some lemonade?"

As soon as those words had left her lips, she realized that she risked sounding way too young.

"Or beer," she added, figuring that she could raid her mother's stash. "Or something even stronger. I know it's early, but one wouldn't hurt, would it? Or it might. I mean, I don't want to make myself sound like some kind of alcoholic, because I'm not. I mean, Mum is. Slightly. Sort of. But that sort of thing doesn't run in families, does it? Or does it?" Sighing, she realized now that she was rambling and embarrassing herself. She took a deep breath and tried to think of some way to change course. "Would you like a cup of tea?"

"Tea would be great, thanks," he replied, getting to his feet.

"Mum's having a day of rest," she explained, keen to change the subject. "She can be a little bit like that sometimes, but I don't really take after her. I'm more like my dad, although he died a while ago." Swallowing hard yet again, she felt as if anything she said was likely to make her sound more and more foolish, and in that moment she really just wanted the ground to open up and swallow her whole. "I'm sorry, what kind of tea do you like?"

"Whatever you've got is fine," he told her, "and -"

Suddenly spotting movement, he turned and looked across the garden. For a moment he wasn't quite sure what he'd seen, but after a few more seconds his gaze began to focus on the garage. He couldn't be certain, but he was starting to think that he might have seen something moving on the other side of one of the dusty windows.

"Are you okay?" Parker asked.

"What's in there?" he replied.

"The garage? No idea. Sorry, but Mum has somehow managed to end up without a key to the place and I haven't gotten around to forcing the door yet. I keep meaning to, but I just never seem to find the time. Why?"

"No reason," he muttered, before turning to her again. "I'm sure it's nothing. So exactly how many different types of tea have you got?"

***

"Lydia Smith was into some seriously dark things," Colin said a short while later, as he and Parker sat at the kitchen table. "Bear in mind that everything I've uncovered has to be taken with a pinch of salt, but she certainly seems to have at least *believed* that she had powers. A lot of other people did, too."

"What kind of powers?" Parker asked.

"Her main focus seems to have been this constant desire to cheat death," he explained. "Depending on the sources you pick, there are even suggestions that she might have done that at least once during her lifetime."

"How?"

"By possessing a new body when her old one was on the brink of failing. Some of the stories might have been classic scaremongering."

"Like an actual, literal witch-hunt?"

"A local girl named Rebecca Barnett went missing in 1889 and was never seen again," Colin told her. "Many years later, rumors started to spread that Lydia Smith had taken her body and possessed her somehow. The facts are lost, there's no way to be certain, but Rebecca's disappearance seems to have been the point when a lot of locals started taking the claims about Lydia a lot more seriously. Thing started to build up and build up, and twelve years later Lydia was suddenly gone from the historical record."

"Doesn't this all strike you as being slightly crazy?" Parker asked. "Scratch that, it's not *slightly* crazy. It's insanity of the highest order. A bunch of local countryside hicks got worked up about some woman living by herself, as if that was some kind of great sacrilege, and then they convinced each other that she had to be a witch. Isn't that one of the oldest stories in history? Isn't it so old that it's almost a cliché? Lydia Smith wasn't a witch. She was just ahead of her time."

"I'm only telling you what my research has uncovered," he continued. "If you want my honest opinion, these stories are usually pretty twisted around, but there's almost always some kernel of truth buried away at their heart."

"So you're saying that Lydia Smith was a murderous witch?" she replied. "Seriously?"

"That's not what I'm saying at all. I just think that, as a historian -"

"An amateur historian," she reminded him, feeling a flicker of irritation. "Sorry, no offense, but you're really just scrambling about in the dirt of this story, and it seems to me like you've just come here today to regurgitate a load of nonsense from the past. This whole situation is starting to feel very... old-fashioned."

"I get where you're coming from."

"And it sounds to me like this Lydia Smith woman was pretty hard done by. How would you like it if a load of local people suddenly thought that you were dangerous? They probably turned on her and stormed out here with their pitchforks raised." She took a look at some of the photocopies for a moment, before sliding them back over to him. "Frankly, I'm a little offended that you'd take their side. Then again, I guess I shouldn't have expected much better from a guy who's probably never even left this village in his life."

"I..."

Colin's voice trailed off for a moment, and then he got to his feet.

"I'm sorry if I offended you," he muttered, clearly embarrassed as he began to gather his things together. "I just thought this was an interesting historical case, that's all."

"Sorry I took it too far," she replied. "Hey, can you stick around? I've been really shitty and the truth is, I could use some company."

"I should go," he told her, barely able to look her in the eye as he headed to the door. "I'm sorry if you think I wasted your time, I was only trying to help."

"But -"

"I won't bother you again," he added, almost tripping over his own feet as he hurried out of the kitchen and rushed into the garden.

"I didn't mean it like that," Parker sighed, leaning back in her chair as she realized that she'd been way too confrontational and even borderline aggressive. "When will I learn to shut my stupid big mouth?"

CHAPTER TWENTY-TWO

SLIDING THE KEY INTO the empty hole on the garage door, Parker jiggled it around for a moment before once again accepting defeat. She'd found a small collection of keys on a ring in her mother's boxes and she'd hoped that one of them might help her get into the garage, but now she was starting to realize that – yet again – she was straight out of luck. She wasn't even sure that the hole was a proper lock at all; she was no expert, but something seemed to be missing.

"There are other ways to open a door," she said after a moment, staring at the hole. "You don't necessarily *need* a key."

She started examining the hinges, figuring that she could perhaps simply lift the door completely out of the way. When that yielded no obvious results, she began to look for some way to entirely remove the handle itself, supposing that she might be able to completely bypass the need for a key. Still having no luck, she took a step back and considered giving up, and then she began to wonder whether she could simply smash her way inside. Sure, the door might be difficult to break, but the window would be easier and there was certainly enough room to wriggle through.

And, crucially, she could always tell her mother later that a bird was responsible.

For a moment she considered scrapping the entire plan. After all, the garage looked pretty rundown and she had no indication that there might be anything truly interesting inside. At the same time, she'd reached this point many times before, only to let herself get distracted; she wasn't a paranoid or superstitious person, but Parker couldn't help feeling that it was almost as if some hidden force was constantly yanking her attention away, keeping her from actually getting into the garage.

But not this time.

This time she was going to get the job done.

Looking around for something she could use, she quickly spotted a rock. She picked it up and glanced at the house, but she knew her mother was safely sequestered in one of the bedrooms and she figured that she probably wouldn't even hear the sound of breaking glass. She stepped a little further back, took a moment to aim, and then she threw the rock, shattering the window with such force that she even shocked herself.

"Damn it!" she gasped.

After a moment, once she was sure that there was no sign of her mother emerging from the house, she stepped over to the broken window and peered through, looking past the remaining shards of glass. She could see a large dark space inside the garage with a fair few boxes piled on either side, but she couldn't really make out much detail. Slipping her phone from her pocket, she switched the flashlight app on and held it up, casting a moderately helpful beam into the darkness.

"Boxes," she muttered under her breath, "boxes and... more boxes."

Spotting something leaning against the far wall, she squinted slightly.

"Doors?" she whispered. "Okay, cool. Some spare doors and -"

Before she could finish, she saw something moving in the shadows. She instinctively took a step back, before forcing herself to look again; aiming the flashlight app's beam across the garage, she saw no movement this time, and she figured that most likely she'd just been a little jumpy.

Feeling as if she needed to see more, she carefully reached through the broken window. Fumbling for some kind of latch on the other side, she had to reach a little further than she'd expected, and she was forced to press her wrist more firmly against a sharp glass edge in the process, although she was able to avoid applying too much pressure. Nevertheless, as she felt some kind of rusty metal contraption on the door's other side, she wondered whether she might be able to get the damn thing open. As she held her phone in her left hand, down by her waist, she stood on tiptoes and tried to reach a little further through the window so that -

Suddenly she felt something bump against her from below, and she looked down just as the black cat took her phone between its teeth and yanked the device away.

"Hey!" she gasped, shocked as the cat ran off across the garden with her phone in his mouth. "Smythe! Stop! You little piece of -"

Pulling her hand back out through the window, she began to set off after him, only to trip and fall hard on the wet grass. Muttering a few curse words under her breath, she raced after Smythe again, even though she'd already lost sight of the wretched creature.

"Come on, bring it back!" she called out. "It's a phone, what do you even want it for? What are you being such a dumb little bastard?"

***

Hurrying around the corner, Parker stopped as soon as she saw Smythe sitting calmly on the grass. The phone was resting on the ground, but as Parker walked over and reached down to pick the device up, she saw to her immense frustration that two cat fangs had neatly pierced the screen.

"Great," she sighed, tapping the button on the side but finding that the phone was dead. "And what do you gain from doing that, huh?" she continued, looking down at the cat. "Seriously, what's the point? It isn't even that shiny!"

Smythe let out a brief meow, as if he was proud of the damage he'd caused.

"You and me are going to end up not being friends at this rate," Parker said with a scowl. "Do you understand me? First the clawing, and now this. If you're trying to piss me off, you're going about it the right way."

Sitting on the step, she tried a few more times to get the phone working again before accepting that it was truly dead. A moment later Smythe wandered over and brushed against her leg, and Parker couldn't help but reach down and pet him.

"I was such a fool earlier," she continued. "Did you hear my conversation with Colin? He was making some perfectly valid points, backed up by historical analysis, and I went off at him like a rocket. I just wish I could get better at thinking before I open my big fat stupid mouth. Then again, that's always been my problem. I'm a loose cannon at times, no matter how hard I try to get myself under control." She paused as tears began to fill her eyes. "And that's how I end up with no friends, talking to some random stray cat."

She sniffed the tears back, before looking down at Smythe again.

"Do you like me, or have I pissed you off as well?" she asked. "The worst part is that -"

Suddenly Smythe surprised her by jumping up and sitting on her lap, purring loudly in the process.

"Okay, that's pretty friendly," Parker pointed out, allowing herself a faint smile. "You know, for a stray cat you seem awfully domesticated. I wish you'd let me get a proper look at your collar, I might actually be able to help. But I guess if you've been alone for a while, you must have learned to be pretty independent. Believe me, I know how that feels." With the cat still sitting a little awkwardly on her knee, she began to stroke his side. "Do you think I should just be friends with animals from now on? For one thing, you won't even understand when I go spouting a load of nonsense, so you can't get offended. And for another, relationships with people are so much harder."

Smythe's purring became a little louder.

"I just don't think that I fit in with human

beings," Parker added, "and -"

Before she could finish, she spotted some lettering on the wall, partially hidden behind a bush. Craning her neck, she tried to read the letters, but after a moment she opted instead to pick the cat up and carry him in her arms as she got to her feet and wandered over to the bush. When she pulled the greenery aside, she was surprised to see what appeared to be a somewhat homemade sign fixed to the wall.

"Smythe House," she read out loud, before contemplating that name for a moment. "Smythe House? Dude, is this house named after you? I thought it was supposed to be called Styre House, but I've got to admit that Smythe House has a much better ring to it."

She stared at the sign for a moment, before reaching out and touching its rough edge.

"Who put this here, huh?" she continued, speaking more to herself than to the cat or anyone else who might overhear her words. "It looks pretty old. You know, arguments with Colin aside, I'm genuinely curious about the history of this house. Do you know anything about that, Smythe?"

She tried to put the cat down, only to find that he was starting to cling to her sweater.

"You're getting a little friendlier than before," she observed. "Does that mean that you've accepted my apology for ruining your peace? Is that it, Smythe? Do you recognize a fellow loser? Are we part of some kind of clan now? Is that it?"

She waited, but the cat was simply purring louder than ever, and after a moment Parker realized that he was showing no sign that he wanted to leave her arms.

"Okay, fine," she added with a smile, sniffing back the last of her tears. "You know what? I think this might be the start of a beautiful friendship. I've got to admit, though, you seem to have warmed to me quite suddenly. What did I do to get you so totally on my side?"

CHAPTER TWENTY-THREE

"OKAY, DO YOU HAVE to... do you really need to sit right there?"

With night having fallen, Parker was at the kitchen table with a bowl of spaghetti and ketchup. Her mother was still holed up in one of the bedrooms, so she'd taken the opportunity to make one of her favorite quick dinners, although these efforts had been somewhat hampered by Smythe's sudden and very pronounced determination to stick as close to her as possible. She'd just about managed to get the animal to go onto the floor while she was cooking, but he'd jumped straight back onto her lap as soon as she'd sat down and now he was purring contentedly.

For her part, while she was glad of the companionship, Parker couldn't help but feel that the cat was now getting just a little too clingy. In fact, as she reached around the animal and spooled some more spaghetti onto her fork, she wondered just what could possibly be behind such an abrupt and dramatic behavioral change.

"You know, you could make this slightly easier," she pointed out. "I don't see how either of us -"

Before she could finish, she heard a heavy bump from the room above. Looking up at the ceiling, she realized that she'd perhaps given her mother far too much leeway. Having not wanted to disturb Alison all day, she now couldn't help but wonder whether she needed to put her foot down once and for all. A moment later she heard a floorboard creaking in the room above, and she couldn't shake the feeling deep in her chest that something was seriously wrong with her mother.

"What would you do in my situation, Smythe?" she murmured. "How would you get such a stubborn woman to admit that there's something wrong with her?"

***

Fumbling with the latch on the inside of the garage door – a latch that Parker had earlier failed to open by just the smallest of margins – Henry Overton finally managed to force the door open before stumbling out into the moonlit garden.

Or, rather, the wretched corpse that had once been Henry Overton achieved this feat.

Barely able to stay upright, with scores of dead mice still stuffed in his body and blood caked around the shapes carved into his chest, Henry took a couple of tottering steps forward while emitting a faint groaning sound from his mouth. He barely knew where he was, barely even knew *who* he was anymore, but he was filled with the overriding urge to somehow get away from the garage. He looked toward the house and saw a light in one of the downstairs rooms, but he knew he couldn't risk staying on the property for even a moment longer. Instead he turned and began to limp away along the drive, finally reaching the street and stopping for a moment to get his bearings.

"I'll be alright," he murmured, reaching up and once more searching for a pulse somewhere deep in his neck, before trying his wrists. "I'll find... I'll find my way home and then I'll fix this. I don't know how, but..."

He began to make his way along the road, before stopping again as he spotted the lights of the village ahead, burning bright through the night air. The road looped round and followed a meandering route into the heart of the village, going all the way around the old church and the attendant cemetery, and Henry realized after a few seconds that he could halve his journey time if he simply went across John McBaringle's potato field. He limped to the fence and looked across the field, although in truth he could see precious little save for various puddles of rainwater in thick ditches all across the land.

For a few seconds Henry debated whether or not this was a wise move, but he quickly reminded himself that above all else he needed to get home as quickly as possible. Resolving to figure everything else out later, he began to clamber over the fence, managing to get about halfway before toppling across the top and landing with a heavy thud on the semi-hard muddy ground below. As he did so, his weight fell entirely on his left wrist for a moment, snapping it heavily to one side.

Letting out a faint groan, Henry realized with a growing sense of shock that his mind was very fuzzy, as if his actual thoughts were barely able to break through. He held his left arm up and saw the hand dangling freely, and when he touched the injured limb he still felt absolutely no sensation at all. A faint wailing sound emerged from his mouth as he realized that something was very wrong with his body, but he still clung to the hope that he could somehow get himself repaired. Deciding not to worry about his broken wrist for now, he began to stumble across the field while fixing his eyes on the lights in the distance and telling himself that soon enough he'd be home.

Then he'd be able to call a doctor, and the police, and anyone else who might be able to fix things. Even a priest, perhaps.

"Help me," he whimpered, rehearsing the lines he planned to say to anyone who'd listen to him once he got home. "For the love of all that's holy, look what's become of me! Won't somebody help me?"

He almost tripped a couple of times on the thick, rugged ground, but somehow he managed to keep going. Swaying a little in the moonlight, he felt his body weakening, and after a few more paces he stopped and put his hands on the front of his chest. Moving the ragged fabric of his shirt aside, he realized that he could feel fresh cold blood oozing from the marks that had been left in his skin; looking down, the light of the moon allowed him to see several dribbles running down to the waist of his trousers, and he began to worry that somehow his body was starting to break apart.

"Wait," he whispered, suddenly struck by a sense of panic as he turned and saw Styre House over his shoulder. He'd been desperate to get away from that place, yet now he felt as if he had to go back, as if each and every step further from the house's boundary left his body weaker.

Almost as if, as he walked, he was losing the magic that somehow kept his corpse animated.

"No," he murmured, as the full enormity of

this horror began to hit his mind, "please, I don't want to have -"

Before he could finish, his right arm fell away, the skin sloughing off what remained of his ragged gray bones. Henry immediately crouched down and, with his remaining hand, picked up his arm and tried to push it back into place, but he could feel that it was still loose. A moment later he felt the same looseness in his left hip, and he looked down just as the leg dropped away, sending him collapsing down into the mud with a heavy grunt.

"Stop!" he gasped, realizing now that his entire body was at risk of falling apart. "I'll come back! You don't have to do this to me!"

Looking toward the house, he spotted a dark silhouette standing at the end of the driveway, watching him from the shadows. This, he realized quickly, was the same rotten woman who'd stood over him in the garage. She had no eyes, so he supposed she wasn't actually 'watching' him, but he reasoned that she might well be sensing his terror and fear.

"Help me!" he sobbed. "Don't do this! I don't want to die! Why are you doing this to me? I never hurt you! I only..."

In that moment his jaw came loose, detaching first from one side and then the other before dropping down and landing in the mud. Henry tried again to cry out, but his tongue merely flapped loosely as blood gurgled in the exposed top of his throat; he reached forward with his remaining hand, but already he could feel his joints becoming looser and after a few seconds he spotted ripples of fire running along his arm.

"Wait," he growled as the flames spread across his body. "I'm not a bad person. Why are you doing this? Please, I -"

Before he could finish, the flames consumed his entire form, burning bright and ripping through what remained of his meat. He tried to crawl forward, but he only managed a few inches before slumping forward, landing with his face against the ground. Somewhere in the heart of the conflagration he was still conscious, as if some otherworldly force was making his mind remain in his body for as long as possible so that he'd feel the absolute maximum amount of pain. Even as his body began to crumble, Henry's mind lingered and he felt the agony of his charred bones dropping down one-by-one onto the muddy ground.

Over by the driveway, the rotten woman stood calmly, sensing the pain as Henry's body collapsed and as the flames finally died out. Down by her feet, meanwhile, Smythe was purring happily, walking back and forth while pressing against her legs.

CHAPTER TWENTY-FOUR

SITTING ON THE SOFA with her feet up on the cushions, Parker stared at the television and tried to lose herself in another mindless reality show. With night having fallen outside, she'd decided to spend the evening numbing her brain, although she couldn't ignore a flicker of concern at the back of her mind.

A moment later, spotting movement, she turned to see the black cat slinking into the hallway and heading toward the stairs.

"Smythe!" she called out. "Hey, do you want to come over here for a fuss?"

The cat stopped and looked at her, as if lost in thought, but after a few seconds he continued on his way.

"No?" Parker continued. "Seriously?

Suddenly I'm not good enough?"

She waited, and a moment later she heard a brief bumping sound coming from upstairs. Looking at the ceiling, she realized that she hadn't seen her mother now for around twenty-four hours, and she could no longer ignore the niggling sense of concern that had been festering in her thoughts all day. The last thing she wanted to do was cause some kind of confrontation, and she felt certain that her mother would come up with another reason to avoid going to see a doctor, but finally Parker got to her feet and told herself that she wasn't going to take no for an answer.

This time, she was going to make Alison see sense.

"Okay," she said, pausing the television before heading out of the room. "Let's see what's really going on up there."

***

"Mum?" she called out as she reached the top of the stairs and made her way across the landing. "I really need you to open this door and -"

Stopping suddenly, she saw that the door – which had remained shut and locked all day – was now partially ajar. Heading over, she looked into the bedroom and immediately saw that with the curtains drawn the place was shrouded in darkness, and as she pushed the door fully open she began to notice a distinctly fusty and rather unpleasant smell.

The door's hinges creaked slightly, but once it was open all the way Parker found herself staring into a disheveled space with her mother just about visible on the bed. Squinting to try to make out what was happening, Parker realized to her surprise that Alison was still resting on her front, with her feet on the pillows and her face leaning over the bottom of the bed. The position seemed strange and unnatural, and Parker was already starting to understand that something was still very wrong.

"Mum?" she said cautiously. "How are you feeling?"

"Hmm?" Alison groaned, sounding barely awake.

"Mum, it's evening now. Listen, you promised that you'd see a doctor if -"

"Wasn't that tomorrow?"

"Mum, you need to see one right now," Parker said firmly, reaching for the switch on the wall. "I'm going to turn the light on and -"

"No!" Alison gasped.

"Why not?"

"I just... I like the darkness."

"That's not a good sign either," Parker pointed out, with her hand still hovering close to the switch. "Mum, enough's enough. You're not fooling me. It's really obvious that you need help, okay? I refuse to stand back and let you get worse and worse." She waited, hoping that she might have made her point, but all she heard was a series of breathless gasps. "Mum, I'm going to turn the light -"

"No!" Alison snapped again. "Parker, be told! This is my bedroom and my house, and I refuse to be told what to do by my own daughter! Will you kindly leave me alone? I'll be... I'll be fine in the morning, I swear. I just need to rest a little more and... wait until tomorrow."

"I'm not waiting a moment longer," Parker replied. "Mum, I'm putting my foot down. You'll thank me later."

Again she waited for a reply, and after a moment she realized that she could hear a purring sound coming from somewhere inside the room.

"Mum, the cat's in here," she added. "You don't even like the cat."

"What?" Alison murmured. "Oh, sorry, Parker I... I think I dozed off for a moment. I forgot you were there."

"This has gone too far," Parker said, switching the light on and then stepping over to the bed. "Mum, I don't care what you think, we've been going round and round in circles but the time has come for me to call a doctor and -"

In that moment, she froze as she saw that Smythe was sitting next to the bottom of the bed, directly beneath the spot where Alison's face was leaning over. The cat was holding one paw up and patting something that seemed to be dangling down, but even with the lights on Parker couldn't quite make out what was happening. She took another step forward, trying to see properly, and then she slowly crouched down so that she could get a better look, at which point she finally let out a horrified gasp as she saw the truth.

Alison's left eyeball was hanging down from its socket, suspended at the end of the optic nerve, and Smythe was casually patting the gooey orb with his paw as if he was playing a game.

"No!" Parker stammered. "What are you doing?"

Smythe turned to her for a moment, before looking at the eyeball again. After a moment his claws extended from his paw, and when he patted the eyeball this time, the sharp tips dug into the surface and caught hard.

"Stop!" Parker shouted, pushing the cat aside, only for his claws to gouge part of the eyeball away.

Pulling her mother back and turning her over on the bed, Parker looked down into her face and saw the left eyeball hanging loose from the edge of the socket.

"It's okay, Parker," Alison whispered deliriously, grinning faintly as if she barely had any strength left at all. "Just let me rest until the morning, and then I'm sure I'll be fine."

"Mum, I'm getting you out of here," Parker said, trying to pull her mother up but finding her strangely stiff. "Mum, can you help a bit? Can you cooperate?"

Before Alison could answer, Smythe jumped onto the bed and started purring again.

"Get away from her!" Parker yelled, shoving the cat so hard that he let out a brief screech as he tumbled back over the side of the bed. "You feral little piece of crap, what the hell's wrong with you?"

"I thought you liked the cat?" Alison murmured. "Parker, do you know what your problem is? You can never just make your mind up and stick to one thing."

"Let's go," Parker said, trying once more to haul Alison off the bed, only to trip and fall, landing hard on the carpet.

She immediately tried to get up, but in that moment she saw a dark stain under the bed, and she realized that the cat had been arranging dead mice in a vaguely human-shaped pattern directly underneath the spot where her mother had been sleeping.

"This is nuts," she said, before getting to her feet and trying once again to pull her mother up. "I don't know what's going on here, but we're getting out of this room right now. Mum, I seriously need you to cooperate."

"Oh, you always make such a fuss over the littlest things," Alison said airily as she slowly got to her feet with her eyeball still hanging from its socket. "I'm sure it's fine, I'm sure it's just a little scratch, that's all."

She stumbled a little, but Parker managed to hold her mother up and led her slowly but surely out onto the landing. Stopping and looking back, she saw that Smythe was starting to follow; grabbing a vase, she threw it at the cat, scaring him away as the glass shattered on the floor.

"What did you do that for?" Alison asked, turning to see the damage. "Darling, your grandmother gave me that vase. It was worth quite a lot of money! I always thought that if the *Antiques Roadshow* ever came nearby, I'd take it along."

"I don't care!" Parker hissed, pulling the door shut and then starting to force her mother over to the top of the stairs. "Mum, I don't know what's going on here but I don't think we should ever have let that cat inside. I'm going to get you away from the house and then you're going to see a doctor and..."

As she began to lead Alison down to the hallway, she couldn't help but glance at the eyeball as it continued to dangle from the bloodied socket.

"I'm sure they'll figure out something to do,"

she continued, "and -"

Before she could finish, all the lights flicked off in the house. Even the hum of the fridge stopped dead, and Parker stood for a moment with her mother, trying desperately to work out what had just happened.

"It's probably just a random power cut," she said finally, although her voice was tense with fear. "Just a... really badly timed random power cut."

"I have to admit," Alison replied, "that I'm feeling a little... woozy. Darling, would you mind if we sit down, at least for a minute or two so that -"

Suddenly she began to fall forward. Parker managed to grab her just in time, holding her up, but she had to support her mother's weight as she slowly helped her down to the hallway and onto the chair in front of the mirror.

"I don't feel quite myself at the moment," Alison continued, sounding increasingly troubled now. "Parker, I think you might have been right. I can't quite think straight but..." Reaching up, she touched her dangling eye with one hand, feeling its surface as her fingers slowly moved to the start of the optic nerve. "What's going on?" she stammered. "Parker, what's this thing hanging from my face? And why can't I see properly? Parker, I need you to be honest and tell me exactly what's going on here."

"Mum," Parker replied, dropping to her knees in the darkness and looking up at her mother's face, "you need help. Really serious help. I still don't know what's going on here, but we can't fix it ourselves, okay? We're way beyond that point. Do you think you can walk to the car?"

"I... I think so," Alison murmured, before looking over at the front door.

"I can drive us to the nearest hospital," Parker explained. "I know I don't technically have my license yet, but I basically know how to drive, and the car's an automatic so that should help. Do we have a plan, Mum? You're not going to argue this time, are you?"

"Me? Argue?" Alison hesitated for a few seconds. "No, of course not, but... Darling, I'm a little confused. Who's that?"

"Who's who?"

"Who's *that*?" Alison continued, pointing past her.

Parker looked over her shoulder, and to her horror she saw a silhouetted figure on the other side of the door's frosted glass. Bathed in moonlight, the figure of a woman was shuffling slowly toward the door as crumbs of dirt and soil fell from her rotten body.

CHAPTER TWENTY-FIVE

"COLIN," MARJORIE SAID AS she sat with her feet up, playing a game on her laptop, "you don't ever feel like you're... missing out, do you?"

"Hmm?"

Looking up from the journal he'd been studying, Colin momentarily felt a little uncertain.

"What do you mean?" he asked.

"Oh, I don't know," Marjorie continued, keeping her eyes fixed on the screen, "it's just that sometimes I think a young man of your age should be out having adventures. Nothing too grand or dangerous, of course, but perhaps a little more exciting than just going to and from the history hub each day."

"There's nothing else I want to do," he told

her.

"And you don't get lonely?"

"No," he continued, although now he was starting to find the conversation a little uncomfortable. "Why would I?"

"I just worry that you don't have enough friends your own age. Everyone you know is either someone who comes to see me, or another of the volunteers at the hub." She finally looked up from the laptop. "I suppose I just worry that you're not going to meet anyone you might take a liking to, if you catch my drift. There must be a nice girl out there for you. Or a boy, I'm not going to judge. All I want is for you to be happy, Colin. Do you see where I'm coming from with all of this?"

"I do," he replied, "but -"

Before he could finish, his phone began to buzz. Sliding it closer, he saw to his surprise that Malcolm Udderford from the shop was trying to get through.

"Hey, Malcolm," he said as he answered. "What -"

"Can you please send someone down to the history hub?" Malcolm replied, sounding weary and annoyed at the same time. "Can't you hear it from where you are?"

"Hear what?" Colin asked.

"The alarm! The burglar alarm, or whatever it is, at the hub has been going off non-stop for the past half hour!"

***

Once he'd finished typing in the code, Colin hit the red button on the front of the alarm, finally silencing the extremely loud siren-like sound that had been ringing out for almost forty-five minutes.

"Don't you get an automated message when that thing goes off?" Malcolm asked, watching from the doorway.

"It should go straight to Henry's phone," Colin told him, flicking the lights on and looking around the room. "He's always the one who deals with stuff like this, but..."

His voice trailed off. He couldn't see any kind of disturbance, although he was unable to shake a strange sense in the back of his mind that *something* was wrong. Or at least different.

"I hope it doesn't go off again tonight," Malcolm muttered, turning and heading out toward the village green. "I swear I can still hear it somehow, echoing in my thoughts. I'm going to have to have a brandy before bed if I'm to have any chance of getting to sleep."

"Sorry again, Mr. Udderford," Colin replied, still watching the room as he tried to work out what his subconscious mind had noticed. He waited for a moment longer, and then he turned the light off and headed out through the door. "I think -"

Before he could finish, he heard the distinctive sound of papers sliding off a table and landing on the floor. He spun round and looked once more into the hub; this time, when he turned on the lights he saw that several papers had indeed fallen off Henry's desk and were now spread out across the floor. He had no idea how that could have happened, and he was also fairly sure that Henry's desk had been bare all day, but as he wandered over and began to pick the papers up he supposed that perhaps Henry had dropped by after the place had closed.

And had left papers on his desk, even though he *never* left anything on his desk overnight.

And then he'd failed to set the alarm properly on his way out, even though he was utterly punctilious about all aspects of the security system.

And then he hadn't responded to the inevitable alert about the alarm.

In fact, all in all, quite a lot of things about the situation weren't adding up.

"Hello?" Colin called out, setting the papers

back on Henry's desk and then listening for a moment. "Henry, are you here?"

He gave him ample time to respond, but in truth he already knew that Henry wasn't the sort of person who'd lurk in the shadows. After a moment, figuring that he should head home, he glanced down at the papers on the desk and saw to his surprise that they concerned Styre House. Picking up a photocopied sheet, he realized that these were images that he'd never seen before. Henry had always jealously guarded the history hub's archive, which he'd insisted he was going to eventually organize and digitize, but now some of the items from that archive had apparently been left out for anyone to see.

Not only left out, but also annotated.

"Henry, have you been writing on these things?" Colin murmured, recognizing the older man's handwriting but wondering why he'd changed his well-honed note-making process.

Checking another page, he saw a grainy photo showing the outside of Styre House, complete with a woman standing on the steps wearing a puzzled expression. A date had been scribbled on the corner of the image, marking it as having been taken in the year 1877, and Colin recognized the face of Lydia Smith from numerous other pictures that he'd seen over the years. For a moment he could only stare at her, imagining her looking back out at him from the slightly grainy image.

He set the picture down and picked up a scrappy old envelope. Tipping the contents out, he found some more photographs, this time originals that had been printed on some kind of hardened board. The edges were frayed and in some cases the images had been touched up and given minor repairs, but the pictures themselves were fairly easy to discern. As he shuffled through them, however, Colin began to realize that they showed a strange and very disturbing scene.

Checking the back, he saw that they were all dated to the year 1901, which was around the time that Lydia Smith was last seen out at Styre House. He looked at a few more of the pictures, and finally he began to understand what he'd found.

These images had been taken on the day when a group of concerned villagers had gone out to 'deal' with the problem of Lydia Smith.

Another photo showed the house's garden, and another showed some kind of shallow pit or grave that had been dug near the door. As he began to understand that the locals had documented their actions, Colin felt a growing sense of fear, which was only compounded when he checked another image and saw a shot of a terrified woman – bound and gagged – being held in place by several men at the edge of the grave. The next image showed her down at the bottom in some kind of makeshift coffin, and the next was similar but with a large amount of dirt having been thrown in on top of her, with a seemingly makeshift gravestone added as perhaps a mocking touch; Lydia's name was carved on the stone, along with the years of her birth and apparent death. Another image showed the grave seemingly filled in, and in that moment Colin began to understand what had actually happened on that fateful day more than a century earlier.

"They buried her alive," he whispered, scarcely able to believe that any of this could be true. "How could anyone do something like that to another human being?"

Another photo showed various men standing proudly next to the filled-in grave, clearly pleased with their day's work. Colin was about to check another photo, but at the last moment he saw that a black cat was visible in the background of the image, watching proceedings from a distance.

"Smythe," he said under his breath. "Obviously not the exact same cat, not unless..."

His voice trailed off, and then as he checked the other photos he found that they mostly featured portrait shots of various local dignitaries. Finally he found one that showed a familiar face; his first thought was that this must be Lydia Smith, since it was the same woman he'd seen being buried alive in the other photos. When he turned the board around, however, he saw an entirely different name written on the back in careful cursive.

"Rebecca Barnett," he read out loud, and now he felt further from the truth than ever. "But if the woman they buried out at the house was Rebecca, then..."

He fell silent as he tried yet again to put all the pieces together. Looking at the image again, he began to doubt himself; was it Rebecca or was it Lydia?

Or – and this seemed like the craziest thought of all – had someone deliberately tried to confuse people by adding conflicting information?

After a few more seconds, he gathered up the papers and photos and hurried to the door, determined to get to the house and warn Parker while there was still time. He turned the lights off, and then he locked the door before rushing off into the night.

The history hub was now shrouded in darkness. Slowly a creaking sound emerged from the far end, and the ghostly figure of Henry Overton stepped forward.

"It took you long enough to work that out," he said somberly, with the tone of a man who'd finally accepted his own demise. "I just pray that you can stop that monster before she kills again."

CHAPTER TWENTY-SIX

"WHO ARE YOU?" PARKER called out, her voice trembling with abject terror as she stepped closer to the door's frosted glass. "What are you doing here? This is private property. You have to leave."

She waited, but all she could see on the other side of the glass was a female figure, picked out by the moonlight. After a few seconds, however, Parker leaned a little closer to the window as she realized that she could also *hear* something out there; the figure seemed to be letting out a series of low gasps, almost as if it was struggling to breathe properly. A moment later the door handle turned, and Parker looked down just as she realized that the figure was trying to get into the house.

Instinctively reaching out, she double-checked that the door was locked and then she took a step back. Somehow, deep down, she knew with absolute certainty that she couldn't let this creature into the house.

"Oh, open the door," Alison said drowsily from the chair nearby, leaning to one side as if she might be about to fall asleep. "Parker, why are you being so highly-strung about all of this?"

"Highly-strung?" Parker replied, unable to hide a sense of shock as she heard the figure still trying to open the door. "Are you serious? Mum, something's really wrong here!"

"Parker -"

"Your eye is literally hanging out!"

"It is?" Reaching up, Alison once again seemed surprised to find her eyeball dangling from the optic nerve. She began to try to push it back in, as if she'd already forgotten that it had ever come out. "Well, that doesn't feel too good," she continued, yet somehow she still seemed fairly untroubled. "Darling, I'm sorry, but I'm feeling ever-so-slightly sleepy and I think I might just take a little... nap right here."

Parker opened her mouth to reply, before realizing that there was no longer any sign of the strange figure outside. Nobody was trying the door's handle, and nobody was standing on the other side of the frosted glass.

"Where did she go?" she whispered, looking around and starting to wonder whether there was any other way that the intruder might gain access. "Mum, are all the windows shut and locked?"

"I don't know," Alison chuckled. "They might be. Or they might not."

"Wait right here," Parker said, hurrying through to the kitchen. "I'm going to find my phone and try to get it working for -"

Suddenly she heard the wild scream of a cat, and something dark and fluffy flew through the air, hitting her in the face. Stumbling back against the wall, she reached up to push the cat away, but at that moment Smythe began to hiss loudly as he dug his claws into her face.

"Get off me!" Parker shouted, pulling the cat away even as his claws dug through her flesh, then throwing him as hard as she could manage against the opposite wall. "I've had more then enough of you right now!"

***

Rushing across the kitchen, Parker reached out and tried to turn the lights on, only to find that the power was still off. Muttering a few curses under her breath, she began to frantically search the room, convinced that her damaged phone had to be somewhere nearby and that it might perhaps work. She wasn't even sure what she was going to say to the 999 operator, but she figured that she just had to get the police out and that then they'd know exactly what to do.

"Come on, you have to be here somewhere," she said under her breath, moving some papers before finally finding her mother's phone. "Thank you!"

She tapped the screen, but she immediately felt a series of thick cuts running through the screen.

"No!" she hissed, trying again and again to unlock the phone, only to find that it seemed to have been scratched to bits, with some of the cuts extending beneath the screen and into the casing.

Finally the screen came to life, barely visible beneath the criss-crossing scratches that had clearly been caused by a cat's claw, but Parker found that she was unable to make any calls. Even the option to make an emergency call was off the table, and after a few seconds she turned and threw the phone across the room in frustration, sending it slamming into the kitchen cabinets and then watching as it clattered down onto the linoleum. The phone had taken a lot of damage, she knew that much, but she'd still hoped it might be teased back to life; now that hope was gone.

"That cat," she sneered. "It's all that cat's fault."

She took a deep breath before looking at the windows. She still couldn't see any sign of a figure outside, but she knew that the threat was unlikely to have simply sorted itself out. After a few seconds, realizing that she couldn't hear any other signs of life in the entire house, she began to make her way cautiously back across the kitchen.

"Mum?" she called out. "Hey, Mum, can you hear me? I think I've got a new plan, okay? We can't stay here, but I think there's something outside that wants to stop us leaving."

Still edging toward the door that led into the hallway, she waited for some kind of response from her mother.

"So here's the plan," she continued. "I'm going to get to the car. I'm not quite sure how, but I'm going to manage it somehow and I'm going to get the engine started. Then you're going to join me. If I have to distract whoever's out there, then I'll figure out a way to do that too. All *you* have to do, Mum, is run to the car when I tell you it's time. Do you think you can manage that?"

Reaching the door, she began to wonder why her mother had said nothing. She figured that perhaps Alison had simply fallen asleep, and when she stopped in the doorway and looked across the darkened hallway she saw that her mother was indeed sitting slumped in the chair.

"Okay, Mum," she said, taking a couple of steps forward, "here's the -"

Stopping suddenly, she saw something moving between her mother's feet. Staring down at the dark mass, she couldn't quite figure it out at first, until finally she realized that her mother's intestines had been pulled out through a hole in her belly and were now dangling down to the floor, where Smythe was entangled in the various loops and tubes, playing with them as if they were nothing more than thick strands of string. As she stared at the horrific sight, watching the glistening intestines shaking in the moonlight, Parker could only try desperately to convince herself that somehow she was mistaken.

Looking up at her, while still wrapped in Alison's guts, Smythe let out a playful meow.

"Parker," Alison groaned, slowly managing to lift her head and look up at her daughter. "I think you might have been right. I think I'm... not doing too well."

"Mum -"

Before she could get another word out, Parker saw a shape approaching the frosted glass. She tried to call out, but in that moment the glass shattered, sending thick shards spinning across the hallway. One of the larger shards sliced straight through Alison's neck, severing her head and sending it tumbling down onto the floor, where it landed in the trail of intestines just as Smythe scurried out of the way.

Turning to look up at her, the cat – with blood caked around the sides of his face and pieces of flesh hanging from his fangs – let out an angry hiss.

"Mum!" Parker screamed, but a fraction of a second later the door cracked open, allowing the rotten figure from the grave outside to finally step into the house.

Stepping back, Parker felt as if her mind was about to break. She tried to tell herself that she was dreaming, that none of this could really be happening, but as she bumped against the bottom of the staircase she watched the dead woman slowly stepping into the hallway. Looking down, she saw her mother's severed head on the floor, resting in a snake-like nest of guts and entrails; she could only stare, unable to process the sight, locked in the hope that somehow everything would reset and the whole world would go back to how things used to be, that her mother would suddenly wake up and insist – as usual – that everything was fine, and that they could all just rewind to a point before they'd ever set foot in Styre House.

"Mum," she sobbed, "please don't be dead. Please, Mum, I need -"

In that moment she screamed as she felt a sharp pain in her ankle. Looking down, she saw that Smythe had bitten her hard; she immediately reached down and grabbed the cat, ripping him away and throwing him out through the broken window, then turning to the rotten woman again.

"Be," the woman gasped, her guttural voice barely emerging from her long-dead throat, "me."

Turning, Parker began to scramble up the stairs, desperately trying to get away. Finally reaching her mother's bedroom, she stumbled inside and threw herself against the door to force it shut, and then she began to sob wildly as she slid down onto the floor. She could hear footsteps beyond the door, making their way up the stairs, but for a moment she could only sob wildly as she thought back to the sight of her mother's severed head on the hallway carpet.

"You can't be dead," she whimpered as tears streamed from her eyes. "Mum, please... I need you!"

CHAPTER TWENTY-SEVEN

HALF AN HOUR LATER – or an hour, perhaps, or even longer – Parker remained in the exact same spot, staring across the darkened bedroom, far too terrified to move a muscle as she replayed the last sight of her mother over and over again.

Another tear rolled down her cheek, but she barely noticed. In her mind's eye she was simply thinking back to the horrific image of her mother's intestines hanging down to the floor. She tried yet again to think of some reason why she was wrong, why her mother might have survived, yet deep down she knew that was impossible. Somehow she also knew that soon she was going to have to scream, that all the pain growing in her chest was going to have to come out, but she wasn't quite ready for that moment just yet. For now, she wanted to freeze time and not move forward, so that in some way she might be able to change everything back and save her mother.

"Mum, if you come back, I'll never say another bad thing again," she whimpered. "I'll never threaten to go to Uncle Rich's place, and I'll never make fun of your healing crystals or your meditation, and I'll never question your latest scheme. I'll be the best, most supportive daughter anyone could ever ask for, even when bits start falling off the house. I'll never be sarcastic again. All you have to do is come back. Please, Mum..."

She fell silent for a moment, waiting even though she knew there was no hope.

And then, finally, she heard a gentle bumping sound coming from somewhere over on the other side of the room. She couldn't see anything moving, but somehow she just *knew* what had happened, and sure enough after a few more seconds Smythe sauntered innocently into view, purring and twitching his tail as he brushed against the side of the bed.

"Don't come near me," Parker snarled, involuntarily clenching both fists at the same time. "I saw what you did to her."

Ignoring Parker's words, the cat made his way closer, acting almost as if he genuinely believed that he'd done nothing wrong.

"Get away from me!" Parker screamed

suddenly, kicking the cat as soon as he was close enough, bringing a pained cry from his throat as he scurried away. "I warned you! If you come near me again, I swear I'll rip your head off!"

She watched as the cat slipped between the legs of the dressing table, and lo and behold after a few seconds the animal squeezed behind the full-length mirror and began to approach once more.

"Are you deaf?" Parker shouted, grabbing the bin from next to the bed and throwing it, hitting the wall and sending Smythe hurrying away again. "What the hell's wrong with you? You just killed my mother, you piece of crap! You..."

As she heard those words leaving her lips, Parker was finally struck by the full enormity of the situation. Her mother's corpse was undoubtedly still down there in the hallway, with her guts hanging out and one eye dangling from her face; Parker knew there was no other way out of the house, that she was going to have to see that awful image at least one more time. She also knew that the rotten woman had to still be somewhere nearby, even if she hadn't actually heard any hint of her for a while now.

Looking around, she tried to spot Smythe but this time there was no hint of his presence. She wanted to believe that he'd finally got the message and had left, but deep down she knew he was still nearby.

A moment later she felt something bump against her elbow, and she turned just as the cat jumped up onto her lap and began to purr once again.

"Get lost!" Parker screamed, picking him up and getting to her feet, then throwing the animal as hard as she could manage across the room, sending him slamming into the opposite wall.

She heard a startled meowing cry and watched as the cat dropped down behind the bed, but she already knew that she hadn't managed to finish him off just yet. Filled with a growing sense of anger, she hurried around the bed just in time to see the cat getting to his feet, and she immediately stepped closer and kicked him hard, sending him skittering under the bed and out of sight.

"You don't give up, do you?" she snarled, hurrying around the bed and kicking him again as he tried to emerge from beneath the other side. "What are you doing? Do I have to finish off all nine of your lives before -"

Stopping suddenly, she realized that the cat seemed to be trying to distract her. She had no idea why that might be the case, at least not at first, but a moment later – hearing the faintest creaking sound – she slowly turned and saw that the door's handle was starting to turn.

"No!" she shouted, racing across the room and throwing her weight against the door, then sliding down onto the floor. "Stay out of here!" she yelled, pushing hard to keep the door shut. "I don't care who you are, but you have to get out of our house!" She started sobbing, and now her body was shaking violently as more and more tears streamed down her face. "Why are you doing this to us?" she whimpered. "We didn't do anything wrong! We didn't do anything to hurt you! Why do you hate us?"

She waited for an answer, even though she knew no answer would come; a moment later she spotted movement just beyond her feet, and she saw that Smythe was yet again making his way closer. This time, however, the cat stopped while he was just out of range, instead preferring to simply purr and watch Parker as she kept her weight pushed against the door. The animal's tail continually flicked, as if he was trying to send some kind of message.

"What are you?" Parker sneered finally. "Are you really a cat, or are you some kind of demon? Because right now, from where I'm sitting, you're not like any cat I've ever encountered. You're evil. You're nothing but pure evil, and I hate you with every fiber of my being, and I swear that even if I don't get out of here alive, I'm at least going to make sure that I take you with me."

The cat simply continued to stare, keeping his eyes fixed on Parker as if he expected her to react in a certain way.

"I should have known that there was something wrong with you right from the start," she continued, as she felt a growing sense of pure hatred starting to rise up through her chest. "I should have sensed it. Mum did, she knew there was something wrong with you. Why didn't I listen to her? Now it's too late, now..." She fell silent for a moment as she once again thought of her mother's corpse down in the hallway. "Now she's dead," she sobbed, "and it's all because of you! Are you happy now? Is this what you wanted?"

Gritting her teeth, she realized two things: first, she was never going to be able to fight her way out of the house, not if there was some kind of monstrous deadly presence out on the landing; and two, if she was doomed, then she really needed to make sure that she took Smythe with her to Hell. Not only for the good of other people, and for the good of anyone else who might one day have the misfortune of setting foot in Styre House, but because of a desire for good old-fashioned revenge.

"Okay," she said finally, shifting onto her knees while using her feet to keep the door shut, "let's try doing this a different way."

She cautiously reached out with one hand, offering an olive branch.

"Kitty, come here," she whispered. "Don't you want a fussing?"

She waited.

No response.

"Do you want to be petted?" she continued, figuring that she was going to have to choose her moment carefully. "Every cat wants some love and attention, right? Doesn't every living thing want to be stroked and fussed once in a while? Sure, you're an evil little bag of shit that seems to have crawled from the depths of Hell itself, but that doesn't mean you don't like having your chin scratched."

Watching the cat's eyes, she saw a hint of anticipation, although she quickly told herself that this might be all in her mind.

"Here, you funny little pussycat," she said, offering a friendly whistle in the hope that she might lure Smythe closer. "There's no need to be scared. I mean, sure, I'm gonna rip your goddamn head off and dropkick it out the window, but there's no way you can possibly know that. So why don't you come here? I promise I'll show you all the compassion and love that you showed my mother. Maybe even more."

She waited, and sure enough the cat began to edge forward. Still purring slightly, Smythe brushed against the side of Parker's right leg; although she knew she had a fair chance of grabbing the animal right now, Parker was determined to make sure that got her revenge, and that meant lulling the cat into a little more of a false sense of security. Now Smythe was almost at her waist, still purring happily as if he'd been thoroughly deceived. She held back, determined to wait until she couldn't possibly miss.

"Just a little closer," she said, reaching over and stroking the cat's side, running her fingers through his jet-black fur as she waited to pounce. She knew that cats lunged for their prey quickly, and she was determined to return the favor. "Maybe one more step," she added softly, trying to sound as friendly as possible even as she bristled at the sound of his arrogant purring. "You can manage one more step, can't you? Or should we meet in the middle?"

She leaned forward, leaving the door unguarded.

"You know," she whispered, still stroking the cat's flank, "you're not so scary. Not really. You might be evil, but... Hell, Smythe, you've really met your match now."

The cat's purring increased.

Taking that as her cue, Parker clamped her hands around his throat, spinning him around before he had a chance to use his claws against her. Getting to her feet despite the pain, she struggled to hold onto the wriggling animal, but already his terrified cries made her think that she might finally have the wretched little fleabag at her mercy. She held him up, momentarily enjoying the sensation of his struggles, and in that moment she felt absolutely sure that she was going to be able to crush his neck.

"Okay, Smythe," she snarled, "time to -"

Suddenly the door burst open. Startled, Parker turned, fully expecting to see the rotten woman from downstairs. Instead, she was shocked to find herself staring at a breathless and clearly very sweaty Colin.

"What are you doing here?" she stammered.

"Your front door's broken!" he gasped. "Wait, that's not what matters. Your mum -"

"I know," Parker replied, as Smythe continued to struggle in her grip, "she's dead. This little bastard's responsible, though, and I'm going to make him pay even if it's the last thing I ever do in my miserable life. There's just one -"

In that instant she saw the rotten woman stepping up behind Colin. She opened her mouth to scream, but Smythe twisted round and lashed out, scratching the side of her face and missing her eye by a matter of millimeters. Falling back, she landed hard on the floor with the cat immediately falling into her chest. Hearing Colin cry out, she turned and looked at the door, only for Smythe to lunge down at the side of her neck and bite hard, sinking his fangs into her flesh and bringing a scream from her lips.

CHAPTER TWENTY-EIGHT

"PARKER, IT'S REBECCA BARNETT!" Colin yelled from the landing. "Or Lydia Smith! It might be Lydia Smith inside Rebecca Barnett or it might not, but either way, she's a witch!"

Trying to pull the cat away, Parker felt his fangs still ripping through the side of her neck. She tried to twist to one side, but the cat's grip was far too tight and after a few seconds she hesitated as she realized that the damn thing might be about to tear out her jugular.

"Parker, the cat's her familiar!" Colin called out, sounding increasingly panicked as he raced into the next bedroom and slammed the door shut, before banging his fists on the adjoining wall. "Parker, can you hear me?"

"Help!" she screamed.

"Parker, their power's intertwined!" he shouted. "If I'm right, you have to find a way to break the connection between them!"

"I don't know how!" she yelled as she felt blood running from the wound on the side of her neck. At the same time, the cat bit down even harder. "It's attacking me!"

"You have to find a way!" Colin insisted, his voice sounding increasingly muffled as he shouted from the next room. "Parker, I think she wants a new body and I'm pretty sure you're the one she's after!"

"Get off me!" Parker hissed, turning to look at the side of the cat's angry face as he continued to gnaw on her neck. "Why are you doing this to me?"

After a moment she spotted the cat's tattered old collar, still clasped in place after so long.

"Maybe she gave that to you," she stammered, as she realized that she only had one chance. "Okay, Smythe, you're not the only one with teeth!"

Pushing past the pain, she twisted her head down until she was just about able to bite the collar. As she felt Smythe's claws digging into her chest, she pulled hard on the leather, trying desperately to chew through the aging material. After a moment she felt the buckle, so she focused her attention there instead, pulling as hard as she could manage even as the pain in the side of her own neck became unbearable.

"Parker!" Colin shouted.

"I'm trying!" she murmured, barely able to get any words out at all. "I just -"

In that instant the buckle broke away. Pulling the collar free, Parker tried to rip it apart, but at that moment she felt Smythe loosen his grip on her neck. Determined to take this chance, she grabbed him and threw him across the room, sending him clattering into the chair next to the dressing table. Sitting up, she put a hand on the side of her neck and felt that although there was a lot of blood, she didn't seem to be actually bleeding out.

A moment later Smythe got to his feet and began to make his way forward once more, still purring and flicking his tail even as Parker's blood glistened all around his jaw.

"Seriously?" Parker snarled. "Don't you ever learn to give up?"

Smythe opened his mouth and began to let out a loud meow, but at that moment the torn collar dropped harmlessly from around his neck. Immediately falling silent, Smythe looked down at the collar, staring at it in disbelief for a few seconds before turning to Parker again. In that moment, Parker felt that for the first time all the smugness had left his stupid little feline face, replaced by something that she could only interpret as fear.

"How does that feel?" she asked. "Are you

_"

Suddenly flames burst across the far wall, consuming the curtains and quickly spreading to the dresser. Horrified by the intensity of this instant inferno, Parker pulled back against the nearest wall and watched as the entire opposite end of the room burned with dazzling fury. As the reflected flames filled her eyes, she saw that the core of the fire seemed to be opening up somehow, revealing an impossible brightness that forced her to start shielding her eyes. A moment later, as she felt the heat starting to build, she saw that Smythe was now frantically digging his claws into the wooden boards as if to stop himself getting dragged into the heart of the flames.

Colin was shouting something in the next room, but his voice was drowned out by the sound of the fire, and by the increasingly terrified cries coming from Smythe's mouth as he was slowly but surely pulled back across the room and into the inferno.

For a few seconds the cat's screams were unbearable, and Parker could only watch as he vanished into the light. A moment later the fire abruptly ended as quickly as it had begun, leaving only a few rippling flames at the other end of the now extremely charred bedroom.

Smythe's collar, meanwhile, was still resting on the floor.

"What the hell?" Parker stammered, unable to understand what she'd just seen. "What the actual..."

For a few seconds she could only stare in stunned silence at the spot where – as far as she could tell – some kind of fiery portal had opened up and dragged the flailing black cat away. Tempted to wonder whether this had been a gateway to Hell itself, Parker felt deep down that no such thing was possible, although at the same time she already knew that impossible things seemed to have a habit of happening lately. She leaned forward and picked up the collar, turning it around in her hands, but a moment later she was jerked back to reality as she heard a heavy slamming sound coming from out on the landing, accompanied by Colin's panicked cries.

Hauling herself up, she managed to reach the door, which she pulled open before stepping through to see the rotten figure trying to force its way into the next bedroom. Unable to see any details in the darkness, she was nevertheless able to smell an unholy stench of death and decay, and a moment later the figure turned and glared at her. Seeing two dark eye sockets staring out from a partially skeletal face, Parker instinctively stepped back until her right foot hit the edge of the staircase's top step. Almost toppling backward, she just about managed to hold herself up as the rotten woman lumbered toward her.

"Parker!" Colin shouted from inside the bedroom. "Are you okay?"

"Not really!" Parker yelled, backing against the wall just as the dead woman reached out and grabbed her by the throat. "Help me!"

Racing out from the bedroom, Colin stopped as soon as he saw the struggle.

"A little *more* help would be good!" Parker gasped as she tried to pull the woman's hand away from her neck. "Don't worry about the cat, it's gone! I think it went straight to Hell!"

"Then their bond should be broken," Colin stammered. "They come as a pair, so when one's been destroyed, the other should weaken."

"Tell *her* that!" Parker hissed.

"I don't understand why it's not already happening!"

Trying to push the woman away, Parker felt dead fingers pressing against the wound on the side of her neck. Unable to breathe, she let out a pained grunt as she began to kick the woman, but a moment later she felt the grip starting to loosen. The dead woman began to emit a low, rumbling groan, and after a few seconds her entire arm broke off, leaving the hand to fall away from Parker's throat and land harmlessly on the floor. The woman stepped back, seemingly shocked by the loss of her remaining arm, but one of her legs fell away and she toppled down onto the floor.

"It's happening!" Colin said, as Parker ran over to join him in the doorway. "She's literally falling apart."

"How?" Parker asked. "Why?"

"Her familiar's gone," he explained. "That means her power's gone too, and it was the power that kept her animated."

They both watched for a moment as the figure continued to crumble, and soon the dead woman fell silent as her head finally slid off and hit the floor, cracking open in the process and spilling out a collection of dusty old brain matter.

"Is she really gone?" Parker asked, unable to quite believe what was happening. "What if she... I don't know, pulls herself back together?"

"She can't," he said firmly. "At least, I don't think so. She was kept going by a spell and now that spell has been broken."

"So all I had to do was break the collar?" she replied. "It was that easy? If I'd broken the collar at the beginning, could I have avoided all of this happening?" She hesitated as tears reached her eyes. "Would Mum still be alive?"

"You can't blame yourself," he told her, reaching out and pulling her close so that he could hug her tight. "But it's over now. Don't worry, that monster and her cat can't ever hurt you again."

AMY CROSS

CHAPTER TWENTY-NINE

Two weeks later...

"IT'S WONDERFUL TO SEE the history hub looking so spick and span," Hilda Worthing said as she stood by the desk and glanced around, her face filled with a sense of wonder. "Colin, I admit that I had my doubts when I heard you were taking over from Henry, but I'm starting to think that a little fresh blood is exactly what this place needed."

She continued to look around for a moment, before suddenly turning to him.

"Oh, I'm so sorry," she stammered, "that must have sounded utterly awful. Of course I'm horrified by what happened to poor Henry. I'd never want anyone to think otherwise."

"It's fine, Mrs. Worthing," Colin replied,

struggling to pay a great deal of attention as he continued to go through some old paperwork. "Think nothing of it."

"Did they find out what dear Henry died of yet?" she asked.

"Not as far as I've heard."

"I can't believe his body was found out there in a field like that," she continued, sounding genuinely perturbed by the whole situation. "I heard he was naked, too." She paused, and then she stepped closer to the desk so that she'd still be heard when she lowered her voice. "You don't think it was a sex thing, do you?"

This, finally, caused Colin to turn to her.

"A sex thing?"

"That's the rumor," she whispered. "That he was out there... in a state of arousal."

"I really don't think that he was," Colin said cautiously.

"There had been rumors about him for a while."

"I'm fairly certain those were completely unfounded."

"But you never know, do you?" she continued, seemingly getting a little hot and flustered now. Reaching up, she adjusted her collar. "You can never be sure what goes on in someone's mind. I liked Henry a great deal, but men especially can be dark horses when it comes to that sort of thing. And why else would he be naked in a field outside the village, if it wasn't something sexual?"

She waited for an answer.

"I really don't know what to say," Colin admitted finally. "I heard he'd been on fire as well."

"I suppose that might explain why he was naked."

"How do you know he wasn't wearing clothes to begin with?"

"Because of the sex club he was in."

Colin sighed.

"I should let you get back to work," Hilda replied, turning and heading to the door. "Oh, and how is that poor young girl doing after the death of her mother?"

"Parker?" He paused for a moment, before forcing a smile. "She's fine. She's just working through it day by day and trying to focus on the future."

"What did the police say happened, again?" Hilda asked, stopping at the door and turning to him. "Some kind of attack by a wild cat?"

"That was their theory, the last I heard," Colin told her. "Apparently Alison's wounds were very much consistent with something like that. They ruled out foul play by a human, at least. And I know there were rumors about Parker, but I hope you realize she's completely innocent."

"Absolutely," Hilda replied. "I never

believed any of that nonsense, not even for a moment. Still, it makes you wonder about Henry, doesn't it? He can't have been acting alone, and you know what that means." She turned and made her way out of the building. "There must be more of them out there. It's probably a sex cult. You never know who might be a member. I shall have to keep an eye out at the next meeting of the fuchsia society."

Colin opened his mouth to reply, but he quickly realized that she wouldn't be able to hear him; besides, he wasn't sure how to respond to such bizarre claims, so instead he looked at the paperwork one last time before checking his watch. In that moment, he realized that he was late for an important meeting.

***

"I don't know," Tom Pullman said, sitting in a corner of the pub as he looked through Colin's notebook, "it's a strange story, I'll give you that much, but it's just not quite believable."

"But that's the whole challenge," Colin pointed out, glancing at his watch again. "Everything I've told you, and everything in that notebook, is true. You have my word. What I'm proposing is a project where I explore the history of the house, and of all the people who've ever lived there, and then I draw in the ghost stuff and everything involving the cat and Mr. Overton, and I try to show how it might really have happened."

"What about this Parker girl?" Tom murmured skeptically. "Is she willing to give her side of the story?"

"I can talk her round."

"You haven't yet?"

"She's still getting over it."

"Then there's the question of public taste," Tom continued. "People won't like it if they think we're peddling a book that's exploitative."

"It won't be, I promise," Colin said eagerly. "I'm not into sensationalism. I'm a historian."

"The two things aren't mutually exclusive. Besides, you don't have any qualifications."

"I might be an amateur, but I know what I'm doing," he explained. "This story has everything. I'm convinced that if I can just research the history of that house properly, and the lives of Lydia Smith and Rebecca Barnett, I can uncover something extraordinary. And I refuse to put any kind of spin on it. My book is going to contain the facts and *only* the facts. History has to be told truthfully."

"And then there's this... cat?"

"The familiar, yes."

"So the cat's evil?"

"It's complicated, and I don't want to commit myself one way or the other," Colin replied, fully aware that he was at risk of sounding like a complete idiot. "Think of Smythe as the selling point. I'm not promising that this book will prove anything supernatural at all, but I *can* guarantee you that people are going to be interested in the story. It's got everything."

"There's a photogenic young girl," Tom agreed, "and a rather horrific death for the mother, and some lurid claims. Then there's the sex pest found dead in the field. It'd be good if you could get interviews with some other members of the cult."

Colin swallowed hard.

"And then there's the cat," Tom added, "and the possibility of something paranormal. I've got to admit, I've been following some of the online whispers about this whole situation and I've found them quite fascinating. Obviously it's one of those classic internet hoaxes, albeit one based on some semblance of truth, but I think we can turn it into something rather useful." He paused again. "It all hinges on the girl, though. If you can bring the girl to me, with her firsthand testimony, then we have a deal."

"She's not some kind of object to be handed over," Colin cautioned, clearly a little uncomfortable with the conversation's latest twist. "I want to work *with* her, so that it's her story that gets told. She's still struggling a lot after her mother's death, and she's refusing to even think about seeing a counselor. I'm not willing to move forward with this project until I'm certain she's ready."

"Don't take too long," Tom said, getting to his feet and grabbing his jacket from the back of a nearby chair. "Six months from now, the world will have moved on. We have to strike while the iron's hot." He slipped a card from his pocket and slid it across the table. "You know how to contact me, Colin, but make it snappy. They used to say that everyone gets fifteen minutes of fame, but now it's barely fifteen seconds. Talk to Polly, get her to understand how lucrative this can be, and call me."

With that, he turned and walked away.

"It's Parker!" Colin called after him, but Tom seemed not to even hear him as he headed out of the pub. "Her name isn't Polly. It's Parker." He picked up the card and looked at it for a moment, before ripping it in half and dropping it into an empty glass. "This was a bad idea," he muttered under his breath. "Parker needs time to heal. The last thing she should be doing right now is going over the whole situation again and again."

"Off to see your girlfriend, are you?" Craig Hurden chuckled at the bar, as Colin made his way past.

"She's not my girlfriend."

"She might as well be, the amount of time you spend with her," Craig continued. "There's no harm in having a little fun on the side, is there?"

"Whatever," Colin muttered, hurrying outside and then stopping for a moment to take a deep breath.

For a few seconds, he felt truly dirty; he'd only agreed to meet Tom Pullman because he'd been promised that the whole project would be tactful, but now he realized he'd been misled. Tom was clearly just looking to sensationalize the case, to turn it from the tragic tale of a girl and her mother to something far more lurid. He watched as Tom's sports car drove away along the tight village lanes, and then he sighed as he checked his watch and saw that he was late. He knew Parker would be waiting for him back at the house, and he wanted to get over there and tell her yet again that everything was going to be alright.

He wasn't sure just yet *how* it was going to be alright, but deep down he felt certain. Somehow he was going to find a way to take the pain from her soul.

CHAPTER THIRTY

STOPPING AT THE FOOT of the steps leading up to Styre House's front door, Colin took a moment to look around. A few journalists had been hanging around lately, trying to suck the blood out of what they believed to be a juicy story, although they seemed to have mostly given up by now. Still, he couldn't help but hesitate for just a few more seconds, keen to make absolutely sure that nobody else was nearby.

After all, he knew that – more than anything else – Parker needed time to get over everything that had happened to her.

Once he was certain that he wasn't being watched, he began to make his way up the steps. He figured that he was going to have to tell Parker about the possible book deal, even if at times he'd managed to convince himself that there was no need; he was growing to like Parker more and more each day, he was even starting to imagine a real future with her, and he figured that he couldn't start a relationship based on lies. In the back of his mind he was still rehearsing different ways to make her understand that the book deal might actually help, and as he stopped at the front door – which was still boarded-up, since nobody had come out yet to fix the damage – he imagined how he might start to bring her around to his way of thinking.

"This'll help you heal," he heard himself saying.

Nope.

Too mercenary.

"You need to get your story out there, to warn others."

No, that'd never fly.

"It's what your mother would have wanted."

He rolled his eyes.

Taking a deep breath, he opened the door and stepped into the hallway. He immediately noticed how quiet and dead the house seemed, and for a moment he wondered whether Parker was even home at all. He listened, but finally he heard the faintest shuffling sound coming from the kitchen and he realized that she was clearly still not feeling too good. He shut the door, and then – as he made his way across the hall – he told himself that perhaps this wasn't the right time to mention the book.

That could wait for another day.

***

"Hey," he said cautiously as he stepped into the kitchen, "what -"

"There you are," Parker replied with a smile, as she took some more items out of the fridge. "I was worried you might be late. How do you feel about a nice lunch?"

"A... nice lunch?" he replied, shocked to see her doing anything other than sitting and sobbing. "Parker, are you -"

"It's such a lovely day," she continued. "I was thinking that we should have something to eat, and then perhaps we can take a walk. I'd love to see how the area has changed."

"But -"

"I'd like to go to Almsford again, too. I never thought I'd ever want to go back there again, but... Well, I had a *lot* of time to think recently, and now I'm quite curious to see what the old place is like. I suppose I'm being a little sentimental, but I can't help myself. I'm particularly curious to see whether they still have that horrible old ducking stool. Oh, and I simply must pop to the churchyard there. It would give me great pleasure to read a few of the names. Esme Walker's, for one."

"Are you okay?" he asked.

"Why wouldn't I be?"

"You just seem a lot more... perky than before."

"Would you prefer it if I sat around moping?" she asked, already carrying various items over to the counter. "I suppose I could give that another try, but it really wasn't achieving anything. I've always thought that the best way to deal with any kind of problem is just to push on through. There's really no alternative."

She started sorting through the various items she'd taken from the fridge, before slowly turning to see that Colin was still staring at her.

"What?" she asked.

"Nothing," he spluttered.

"How was the village?" she continued, and now she sounded just a little irritated. "I bet they're all still loving the gossip, aren't they? Some things never change." She hesitated for a moment, seemingly lost in thought. "I bet they're all still pretending to be good people, too. Probably going to church, fattening themselves up on a sense of their own importance, never once stopping to think about all the awful things they've done. As for their ancestors, they probably got away with it all. They're probably remembered as pillars of the community."

She let out a sigh, before shaking her head and forcing a slightly unnatural smile.

"Then again," she added, "I'm not here to dwell on the past. I'm far more interested in the future. Aren't you?"

"I -"

Before he could finish, Colin felt something brush against his leg. He looked down just in time to see Smythe slinking past, and he watched with a growing sense of shock as the cat jumped up onto the counter and made his way over to Parker.

"There you are," she said as she stroked Smythe's side, causing him to purr loudly. "I was starting to worry."

"Parker," Colin said cautiously, "what's going on here?"

"Are you hungry?" she continued, clearly still speaking to the cat. "You must be, after all your exertions. Don't worry, I'll find something really nice for you." She held up a packet of sliced cheese. "Some of these things are so bizarre," she murmured, peering at the cheese more closely, "but I've always been adaptable. You know that about me, Smythe, don't you? I'm sure you remember. I'm not one to live in the past or shy away from change."

"Parker?" Colin said, raising a skeptical eyebrow.

"I missed you, you know," she added,

leaning down and kissing the top of Smythe's head. "I always believed in you, though. I never for one moment worried that you'd let me down. We've always been a pretty good team, haven't we? Ever since the day Father brought you home, we've always had this kind of... connection. Do you remember how poorly you were at first? Do you remember how I nursed you back to health? Oh, but my little darling, you must be absolutely starving. I know you like to hunt, but how about I find you an extra snack so that you can get your strength back?"

She reached a hand out toward the window, and a moment later a small bird slammed into the glass before dropping down out of sight. Smythe immediately jumped down off the counter and made his way back past Colin, quickly heading out into the garden.

Walking over to the window, Colin looked out just in time to see that the bird was still just about alive. Twitching on the grass, the poor thing seemed to be trying to fly again, but Smythe had already made his way over. Colin winced as he saw the cat extend a single claw, which sliced into the bird's chest and lifted its quivering body up from the ground. Smythe stared at the bird as it struggled, before leaning closer and biting its head off, letting blood gush out from the stump.

"Parker," Colin said nervously, unable to tear his gaze away as Smythe chewed on the bird's corpse, "how..."

His voice trailed off for a few seconds.

"He's back," he stammered. "I thought you said he was dragged into the flames. How is he back? When you described it, you made it sound like he'd been dragged down to the depths of Hell."

"Yes," Parker replied airily, "but I wouldn't worry your pretty little head about that too much." She paused for a moment. "He's always had excellent recall."

Colin turned to find her standing right behind him, looking into his eyes with a determined glare that suggested she found something highly amusing. As he heard the sound of Smythe crunching through the bird's bones outside, Colin stared back at Parker and realized for the first time that he was seeing something different in her eyes. Something colder. Something harder. Something new, or...

Or *someone* new.

"It's so good to be here," she said softly. "You have no idea how long I waited. I was awake for it all, you know. For every awful second. And now..." Reaching out, she touched the side of his face, caressing his skin as if she'd been starved of human contact. "I won't let them do it to me again," she purred. "This time, if anyone comes to try to take me down, I won't be so patient and I certainly won't show them any mercy." She leaned even closer, as if she was about to kiss him on the lips. "This time," she added, "I'm going to take what's rightfully mine."

***

Outside on the lawn, Smythe bit down hard on the bird's chest, sending more blood bursting from the tiny corpse as its bones snapped. A moment later, hearing a thud coming from inside the house, he momentarily looked up at the window; still holding the bloodied bird in his jaws, Smythe watched for a moment before Parker stepped into view and smiled.

Settling down on the sun-dappled lawn, Smythe began to pull the bird's body apart, savoring the warm blood gushing into his mouth. As he did so – content that after so many years he'd finally managed to get his mistress back, and untroubled by a few patches of singed fur – he began to let out a low, happy purr.

THE HAUNTING OF STYRE HOUSE

AMY CROSS

Next in this series

THE CURSE OF BLOODACRE FARM
(THE SMYTHE TRILOGY BOOK 2)

Many years before the horrific events at Styre House, a young girl named Lydia Smith discovers a mysterious set of books filled with dark powers. As she begins to learn the secrets of these books, however, she inadvertently unleashes powers beyond her wildest imagination, powers that shatter the barrier between life and death.

Trapped in a life of misery, Lydia has never thought much about the outside world. All she does every day is care for her sick mother and try to avoid her cruel, bitter father. Her new powers offer a way out, but first Lydia must learn to control the forces she has begun to summon. Fortunately she has help from a set of reanimated bones that rise from the garden, but can anything truly prepare Lydia for the terror that awaits?

And how does she end up as the bitter, monstrous creature that years later will rise from the dirt of Styre House?

AMY CROSS

Also by Amy Cross

1689
(The Haunting of Hadlow House book 1)

All Richard Hadlow wants is a happy family and a peaceful home. Having built the perfect house deep in the Kent countryside, now all he needs is a wife. He's about to discover, however, that even the most perfectly-laid plans can go horribly and tragically wrong.

The year is 1689 and England is in the grip of turmoil. A pretender is trying to take the throne, but Richard has no interest in the affairs of his country. He only cares about finding the perfect wife and giving her a perfect life. But someone – or something – at his newly-built house has other ideas. Is Richard's new life about to be destroyed forever?

Hadlow House is brand new, but already there are strange whispers in the corridors and unexplained noises at night. Has Richard been unlucky, is his new wife simply imagining things, or is a dark secret from the past about to rise up and deliver Richard's worst nightmare? Who wins when the past and the present collide?

AMY CROSS

Also by Amy Cross

The Haunting of Nelson Street
(The Ghosts of Crowford book 1)

Crowford, a sleepy coastal town in the south of England, might seem like an oasis of calm and tranquility. Beneath the surface, however, dark secrets are waiting to claim fresh victims, and ghostly figures plot revenge.

Having finally decided to leave the hustle of London, Daisy and Richard Johnson buy two houses on Nelson Street, a picturesque street in the center of Crowford. One house is perfect and ready to move into, while the other is a fire-ravaged wreck that needs a lot of work. They figure they have plenty of time to work on the damaged house while Daisy recovers from a traumatic event.

Soon, they discover that the two houses share a common link to the past. Something awful once happened on Nelson Street, something that shook the town to its core.

AMY CROSS

Also by Amy Cross

The Revenge of the Mercy Belle
(The Ghosts of Crowford book 2)

The year is 1950, and a great tragedy has struck the town of Crowford. Three local men have been killed in a storm, after their fishing boat the Mercy Belle sank. A mysterious fourth man, however, was rescue. Nobody knows who he is, or what he was doing on the Mercy Belle... and the man has lost his memory.

Five years later, messages from the dead warn of impending doom for Crowford. The ghosts of the Mercy Belle's crew demand revenge, and the whole town is being punished. The fourth man still has no memory of his previous existence, but he's married now and living under the named Edward Smith. As Crowford's suffering continues, the locals begin to turn against him.

What really happened on the night the Mercy Belle sank? Did the fourth man cause the tragedy? And will Crowford survive if this man is not sent to meet his fate?

Also by Amy Cross

The Devil, the Witch and the Whore
(The Deal book 1)

"Leave the forest alone. Whatever's out there, just let it be. Don't make it angry."

When a horrific discovery is made at the edge of town, Sheriff James Kopperud realizes the answers he seeks might be waiting beyond in the vast forest. But everybody in the town of Deal knows that there's something out there in the forest, something that should never be disturbed. A deal was made long ago, a deal that was supposed to keep the town safe. And if he insists on investigating the murder of a local girl, James is going to have to break that deal and head out into the wilderness.

Meanwhile, James has no idea that his estranged daughter Ramsey has returned to town. Ramsey is running from something, and she thinks she can find safety in the vast tunnel system that runs beneath the forest. Before long, however, Ramsey finds herself coming face to face with creatures that hide in the shadows. One of these creatures is known as the devil, and another is known as the witch. They're both waiting for the whore to arrive, but for very different reasons. And soon Ramsey is offered a terrible deal, one that could save or destroy the entire town, and maybe even the world.

Also by Amy Cross

If You Didn't Like Me Then, You Probably Won't Like Me Now

One year ago, Sheryl and her friends did something bad. Really bad. They ritually humiliated local girl Rachel Ritter, before posting the video online for all to see. After that night, Rachel left town and was never seen again. Until now.

Late one night, Sheryl and her friends realize that Rachel's back. At first they think there's on reason to be concerned, but a series of strange events soon convince them that they need to be worried. On the outside, Rachel acts as if all is forgiven, but she's hiding a shocking secret that soon starts to have deadly consequences.

By the time they understand the full horror of Rachel's plans, Sheryl and her friends might be too late to save themselves. Is Rachel really out for revenge? What does she have in store for her tormentors? And just how far is she willing to go? Would she, for example, do something that nobody in all of human history has ever managed to achieve?

If You Didn't Like Me Then, You Probably Won't Like Me Now is a horror novel about the surprising nature of revenge, about the power of hatred, and about the future of humanity.

Also by Amy Cross

The Soul Auction

"I saw a woman on the beach. I watched her face a demon."

Thirty years after her mother's death, Alice Ashcroft is drawn back to the coastal English town of Curridge. Somebody in Curridge has been reviewing Alice's novels online, and in those reviews there have been tantalizing hints at a hidden truth. A truth that seems to be linked to her dead mother.

"Thirty years ago, there was a soul auction."

Once she reaches Curridge, Alice finds strange things happening all around her. Something attacks her car. A figure watches her on the beach at night. And when she tries to find the person who has been reviewing her books, she makes a horrific discovery.

What really happened to Alice's mother thirty years ago? Who was she talking to, just moments before dropping dead on the beach? What caused a huge rockfall that nearly tore a nearby cliff-face in half? And what sinister presence is lurking in the grounds of the local church?

BOOKS BY AMY CROSS

1. Dark Season: The Complete First Series (2011)
2. Werewolves of Soho (Lupine Howl book 1) (2012)
3. Werewolves of the Other London (Lupine Howl book 2) (2012)
4. Ghosts: The Complete Series (2012)
5. Dark Season: The Complete Second Series (2012)
6. The Children of Black Annis (Lupine Howl book 3) (2012)
7. Destiny of the Last Wolf (Lupine Howl book 4) (2012)
8. Asylum (The Asylum Trilogy book 1) (2012)
9. Dark Season: The Complete Third Series (2013)
10. Devil's Briar (2013)
11. Broken Blue (The Broken Trilogy book 1) (2013)
12. The Night Girl (2013)
13. Days 1 to 4 (Mass Extinction Event book 1) (2013)
14. Days 5 to 8 (Mass Extinction Event book 2) (2013)
15. The Library (The Library Chronicles book 1) (2013)
16. American Coven (2013)
17. Werewolves of Sangreth (Lupine Howl book 5) (2013)
18. Broken White (The Broken Trilogy book 2) (2013)
19. Grave Girl (Grave Girl book 1) (2013)
20. Other People's Bodies (2013)
21. The Shades (2013)
22. The Vampire's Grave and Other Stories (2013)
23. Darper Danver: The Complete First Series (2013)
24. The Hollow Church (2013)
25. The Dead and the Dying (2013)
26. Days 9 to 16 (Mass Extinction Event book 3) (2013)
27. The Girl Who Never Came Back (2013)
28. Ward Z (The Ward Z Series book 1) (2013)
29. Journey to the Library (The Library Chronicles book 2) (2014)
30. The Vampires of Tor Cliff Asylum (2014)
31. The Family Man (2014)
32. The Devil's Blade (2014)
33. The Immortal Wolf (Lupine Howl book 6) (2014)
34. The Dying Streets (Detective Laura Foster book 1) (2014)
35. The Stars My Home (2014)
36. The Ghost in the Rain and Other Stories (2014)
37. Ghosts of the River Thames (The Robinson Chronicles book 1) (2014)
38. The Wolves of Cur'eath (2014)
39. Days 46 to 53 (Mass Extinction Event book 4) (2014)
40. The Man Who Saw the Face of the World (2014)
41. The Art of Dying (Detective Laura Foster book 2) (2014)

42. Raven Revivals (Grave Girl book 2) (2014)
43. Arrival on Thaxos (Dead Souls book 1) (2014)
44. Birthright (Dead Souls book 2) (2014)
45. A Man of Ghosts (Dead Souls book 3) (2014)
46. The Haunting of Hardstone Jail (2014)
47. A Very Respectable Woman (2015)
48. Better the Devil (2015)
49. The Haunting of Marshall Heights (2015)
50. Terror at Camp Everbee (The Ward Z Series book 2) (2015)
51. Guided by Evil (Dead Souls book 4) (2015)
52. Child of a Bloodied Hand (Dead Souls book 5) (2015)
53. Promises of the Dead (Dead Souls book 6) (2015)
54. Days 54 to 61 (Mass Extinction Event book 5) (2015)
55. Angels in the Machine (The Robinson Chronicles book 2) (2015)
56. The Curse of Ah-Qal's Tomb (2015)
57. Broken Red (The Broken Trilogy book 3) (2015)
58. The Farm (2015)
59. Fallen Heroes (Detective Laura Foster book 3) (2015)
60. The Haunting of Emily Stone (2015)
61. Cursed Across Time (Dead Souls book 7) (2015)
62. Destiny of the Dead (Dead Souls book 8) (2015)
63. The Death of Jennifer Kazakos (Dead Souls book 9) (2015)
64. Alice Isn't Well (Death Herself book 1) (2015)
65. Annie's Room (2015)
66. The House on Everley Street (Death Herself book 2) (2015)
67. Meds (The Asylum Trilogy book 2) (2015)
68. Take Me to Church (2015)
69. Ascension (Demon's Grail book 1) (2015)
70. The Priest Hole (Nykolas Freeman book 1) (2015)
71. Eli's Town (2015)
72. The Horror of Raven's Briar Orphanage (Dead Souls book 10) (2015)
73. The Witch of Thaxos (Dead Souls book 11) (2015)
74. The Rise of Ashalla (Dead Souls book 12) (2015)
75. Evolution (Demon's Grail book 2) (2015)
76. The Island (The Island book 1) (2015)
77. The Lighthouse (2015)
78. The Cabin (The Cabin Trilogy book 1) (2015)
79. At the Edge of the Forest (2015)
80. The Devil's Hand (2015)
81. The 13th Demon (Demon's Grail book 3) (2016)
82. After the Cabin (The Cabin Trilogy book 2) (2016)
83. The Border: The Complete Series (2016)
84. The Dead Ones (Death Herself book 3) (2016)

THE HAUNTING OF STYRE HOUSE

85. A House in London (2016)
86. Persona (The Island book 2) (2016)
87. Battlefield (Nykolas Freeman book 2) (2016)
88. Perfect Little Monsters and Other Stories (2016)
89. The Ghost of Shapley Hall (2016)
90. The Blood House (2016)
91. The Death of Addie Gray (2016)
92. The Girl With Crooked Fangs (2016)
93. Last Wrong Turn (2016)
94. The Body at Auercliff (2016)
95. The Printer From Hell (2016)
96. The Dog (2016)
97. The Nurse (2016)
98. The Haunting of Blackwych Grange (2016)
99. Twisted Little Things and Other Stories (2016)
100. The Horror of Devil's Root Lake (2016)
101. The Disappearance of Katie Wren (2016)
102. B&B (2016)
103. The Bride of Ashbyrn House (2016)
104. The Devil, the Witch and the Whore (The Deal Trilogy book 1) (2016)
105. The Ghosts of Lakeforth Hotel (2016)
106. The Ghost of Longthorn Manor and Other Stories (2016)
107. Laura (2017)
108. The Murder at Skellin Cottage (Jo Mason book 1) (2017)
109. The Curse of Wetherley House (2017)
110. The Ghosts of Hexley Airport (2017)
111. The Return of Rachel Stone (Jo Mason book 2) (2017)
112. Haunted (2017)
113. The Vampire of Downing Street and Other Stories (2017)
114. The Ash House (2017)
115. The Ghost of Molly Holt (2017)
116. The Camera Man (2017)
117. The Soul Auction (2017)
118. The Abyss (The Island book 3) (2017)
119. Broken Window (The House of Jack the Ripper book 1) (2017)
120. In Darkness Dwell (The House of Jack the Ripper book 2) (2017)
121. Cradle to Grave (The House of Jack the Ripper book 3) (2017)
122. The Lady Screams (The House of Jack the Ripper book 4) (2017)
123. A Beast Well Tamed (The House of Jack the Ripper book 5) (2017)
124. Doctor Charles Grazier (The House of Jack the Ripper book 6) (2017)
125. The Raven Watcher (The House of Jack the Ripper book 7) (2017)
126. The Final Act (The House of Jack the Ripper book 8) (2017)
127. Stephen (2017)

128. The Spider (2017)
129. The Mermaid's Revenge (2017)
130. The Girl Who Threw Rocks at the Devil (2018)
131. Friend From the Internet (2018)
132. Beautiful Familiar (2018)
133. One Night at a Soul Auction (2018)
134. 16 Frames of the Devil's Face (2018)
135. The Haunting of Caldgrave House (2018)
136. Like Stones on a Crow's Back (The Deal Trilogy book 2) (2018)
137. Room 9 and Other Stories (2018)
138. The Gravest Girl of All (Grave Girl book 3) (2018)
139. Return to Thaxos (Dead Souls book 13) (2018)
140. The Madness of Annie Radford (The Asylum Trilogy book 3) (2018)
141. The Haunting of Briarwych Church (Briarwych book 1) (2018)
142. I Just Want You To Be Happy (2018)
143. Day 100 (Mass Extinction Event book 6) (2018)
144. The Horror of Briarwych Church (Briarwych book 2) (2018)
145. The Ghost of Briarwych Church (Briarwych book 3) (2018)
146. Lights Out (2019)
147. Apocalypse (The Ward Z Series book 3) (2019)
148. Days 101 to 108 (Mass Extinction Event book 7) (2019)
149. The Haunting of Daniel Bayliss (2019)
150. The Purchase (2019)
151. Harper's Hotel Ghost Girl (Death Herself book 4) (2019)
152. The Haunting of Aldburn House (2019)
153. Days 109 to 116 (Mass Extinction Event book 8) (2019)
154. Bad News (2019)
155. The Wedding of Rachel Blaine (2019)
156. Dark Little Wonders and Other Stories (2019)
157. The Music Man (2019)
158. The Vampire Falls (Three Nights of the Vampire book 1) (2019)
159. The Other Ann (2019)
160. The Butcher's Husband and Other Stories (2019)
161. The Haunting of Lannister Hall (2019)
162. The Vampire Burns (Three Nights of the Vampire book 2) (2019)
163. Days 195 to 202 (Mass Extinction Event book 9) (2019)
164. Escape From Hotel Necro (2019)
165. The Vampire Rises (Three Nights of the Vampire book 3) (2019)
166. Ten Chimes to Midnight: A Collection of Ghost Stories (2019)
167. The Strangler's Daughter (2019)
168. The Beast on the Tracks (2019)
169. The Haunting of the King's Head (2019)
170. I Married a Serial Killer (2019)

THE HAUNTING OF STYRE HOUSE

171. Your Inhuman Heart (2020)
172. Days 203 to 210 (Mass Extinction Event book 10) (2020)
173. The Ghosts of David Brook (2020)
174. Days 349 to 356 (Mass Extinction Event book 11) (2020)
175. The Horror at Criven Farm (2020)
176. Mary (2020)
177. The Middlewych Experiment (Chaos Gear Annie book 1) (2020)
178. Days 357 to 364 (Mass Extinction Event book 12) (2020)
179. Day 365: The Final Day (Mass Extinction Event book 13) (2020)
180. The Haunting of Hathaway House (2020)
181. Don't Let the Devil Know Your Name (2020)
182. The Legend of Rinth (2020)
183. The Ghost of Old Coal House (2020)
184. The Root (2020)
185. I'm Not a Zombie (2020)
186. The Ghost of Annie Close (2020)
187. The Disappearance of Lonnie James (2020)
188. The Curse of the Langfords (2020)
189. The Haunting of Nelson Street (The Ghosts of Crowford 1) (2020)
190. Strange Little Horrors and Other Stories (2020)
191. The House Where She Died (2020)
192. The Revenge of the Mercy Belle (The Ghosts of Crowford 2) (2020)
193. The Ghost of Crowford School (The Ghosts of Crowford book 3) (2020)
194. The Haunting of Hardlocke House (2020)
195. The Cemetery Ghost (2020)
196. You Should Have Seen Her (2020)
197. The Portrait of Sister Elsa (The Ghosts of Crowford book 4) (2021)
198. The House on Fisher Street (2021)
199. The Haunting of the Crowford Hoy (The Ghosts of Crowford 5) (2021)
200. Trill (2021)
201. The Horror of the Crowford Empire (The Ghosts of Crowford 6) (2021)
202. Out There (The Ted Armitage Trilogy book 1) (2021)
203. The Nightmare of Crowford Hospital (The Ghosts of Crowford 7) (2021)
204. Twist Valley (The Ted Armitage Trilogy book 2) (2021)
205. The Great Beyond (The Ted Armitage Trilogy book 3) (2021)
206. The Haunting of Edward House (2021)
207. The Curse of the Crowford Grand (The Ghosts of Crowford 8) (2021)
208. How to Make a Ghost (2021)
209. The Ghosts of Crossley Manor (The Ghosts of Crowford 9) (2021)
210. The Haunting of Matthew Thorne (2021)
211. The Siege of Crowford Castle (The Ghosts of Crowford 10) (2021)
212. Daisy: The Complete Series (2021)
213. Bait (Bait book 1) (2021)

214. Origin (Bait book 2) (2021)
215. Heretic (Bait book 3) (2021)
216. Anna's Sister (2021)
217. The Haunting of Quist House (The Rose Files 1) (2021)
218. The Haunting of Crowford Station (The Ghosts of Crowford 11) (2022)
219. The Curse of Rosie Stone (2022)
220. The First Order (The Chronicles of Sister June book 1) (2022)
221. The Second Veil (The Chronicles of Sister June book 2) (2022)
222. The Graves of Crowford Rise (The Ghosts of Crowford 12) (2022)
223. Dead Man: The Resurrection of Morton Kane (2022)
224. The Third Beast (The Chronicles of Sister June book 3) (2022)
225. The Legend of the Crossley Stag (The Ghosts of Crowford 13) (2022)
226. One Star (2022)
227. The Ghost in Room 119 (2022)
228. The Fourth Shadow (The Chronicles of Sister June book 4) (2022)
229. The Soldier Without a Past (Dead Souls book 14) (2022)
230. The Ghosts of Marsh House (2022)
231. Wax: The Complete Series (2022)
232. The Phantom of Crowford Theatre (The Ghosts of Crowford 14) (2022)
233. The Haunting of Hurst House (Mercy Willow book 1) (2022)
234. Blood Rains Down From the Sky (The Deal Trilogy book 3) (2022)
235. The Spirit on Sidle Street (Mercy Willow book 2) (2022)
236. The Ghost of Gower Grange (Mercy Willow book 3) (2022)
237. The Curse of Clute Cottage (Mercy Willow book 4) (2022)
238. The Haunting of Anna Jenkins (Mercy Willow book 5) (2023)
239. The Death of Mercy Willow (Mercy Willow book 6) (2023)
240. Angel (2023)
241. The Eyes of Maddy Park (2023)
242. If You Didn't Like Me Then, You Probably Won't Like Me Now (2023)
243. The Terror of Torfork Tower (Mercy Willow 7) (2023)
244. The Phantom of Payne Priory (Mercy Willow 8) (2023)
245. The Devil on Davis Drive (Mercy Willow 9) (2023)
246. The Haunting of the Ghost of Tom Bell (Mercy Willow 10) (2023)
247. The Other Ghost of Gower Grange (Mercy Willow 11) (2023)
248. The Haunting of Olive Atkins (Mercy Willow 12) (2023)
249. The End of Marcy Willow (Mercy Willow 13) (2023)
250. The Last Haunted House on Mars and Other Stories (2023)
251. 1689 (The Haunting of Hadlow House 1) (2023)
252. 1722 (The Haunting of Hadlow House 2) (2023)
253. 1775 (The Haunting of Hadlow House 3) (2023)
254. The Terror of Crowford Carnival (The Ghosts of Crowford 15) (2023)
255. 1800 (The Haunting of Hadlow House 4) (2023)
256. 1837 (The Haunting of Hadlow House 5) (2023)

257. 1885 (The Haunting of Hadlow House 6) (2023)
258. 1901 (The Haunting of Hadlow House 7) (2023)
259. 1918 (The Haunting of Hadlow House 8) (2023)
260. The Secret of Adam Grey (The Ghosts of Crowford 16) (2023)
261. 1926 (The Haunting of Hadlow House 9) (2023)
262. 1939 (The Haunting of Hadlow House 10) (2023)
263. The Fifth Tomb (The Chronicles of Sister June 5) (2023)
264. 1966 (The Haunting of Hadlow House 11) (2023)
265. 1999 (The Haunting of Hadlow House 12) (2023)
266. The Hauntings of Mia Rush (2023)
267. 2024 (The Haunting of Hadlow House 13) (2024)
268. The Sixth Window (The Chronicles of Sister June 6) (2024)
269. Little Miss Dead (The Horrors of Sobolton 1) (2024)
270. Swan Territory (The Horrors of Sobolton 2) (2024)
271. Dead Widow Road (The Horrors of Sobolton 3) (2024)
272. The Haunting of Stryke Brothers (The Ghosts of Crowford 17) (2024)
273. In a Lonely Grave (The Horrors of Sobolton 4) (2024)
274. Electrification (The Horrors of Sobolton 5) (2024)
275. Man on the Moon (The Horrors of Sobolton 6) (2024)
276. The Haunting of Styre House (The Smythe Trilogy 1) (2024)
277. The Curse of Bloodacre Farm (The Smythe Trilogy 2) (2024)
278. The Horror of Styre House (The Smythe Trilogy 3) (2024)
279. Cry of the Wolf (The Horrors of Sobolton 7) (2024)

AMY CROSS

For more information, visit:

www.amycross.com

AMY CROSS

Printed in Great Britain
by Amazon